MARSUPILAMI

Bamboo Baby Blues

Artwork: **Batem**
Script: **Greg**
Directed by: **Franquin**
Colours: **Leonardo**

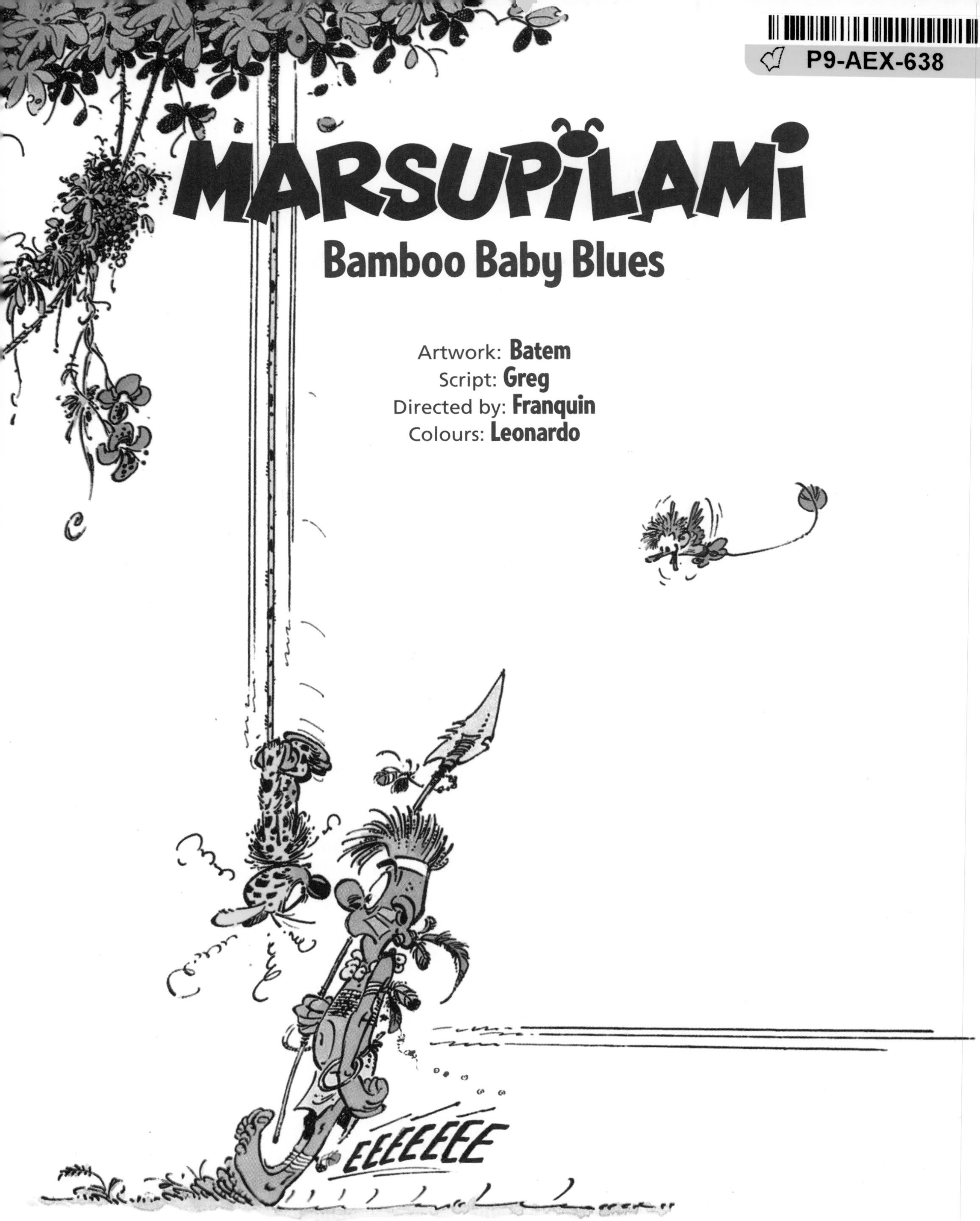
EEEEEEE

9th CINEBOOK
The 9th Art Publisher

Original title: Le bébé du bout du monde
Original edition: © Dupuis, Dargaud-Lombard s.a. 2017 by Franquin, Greg & Batem
www.marsupilami.com
English translation: © 2017 Cinebook Ltd
Translator: Jerome Saincantin
Editor: Erica Olson Jeffrey
Lettering and text layout: Design Amorandi
Printed in Spain by EGEDSA
This edition first published in Great Britain in 2017 by
Cinebook Ltd
56 Beech Avenue
Canterbury, Kent
CT4 7TA
www.cinebook.com
A CIP catalogue record for this book
is available from the British Library
ISBN 978-1-84918-364-2

9th CINEBOOK
The 9th Art Publisher

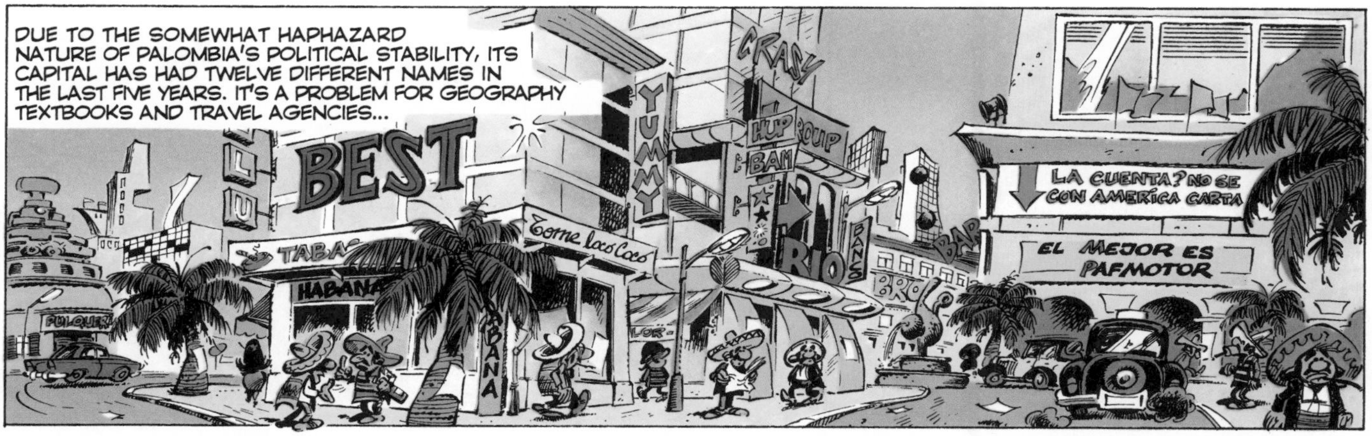
DUE TO THE SOMEWHAT HAPHAZARD NATURE OF PALOMBIA'S POLITICAL STABILITY, ITS CAPITAL HAS HAD TWELVE DIFFERENT NAMES IN THE LAST FIVE YEARS. IT'S A PROBLEM FOR GEOGRAPHY TEXTBOOKS AND TRAVEL AGENCIES...
BEST
YUMMY
LA CUENTA? NO SE CON AMERICA CARTA
EL MEJOR ES PAFMOTOR
HABANA
RIO

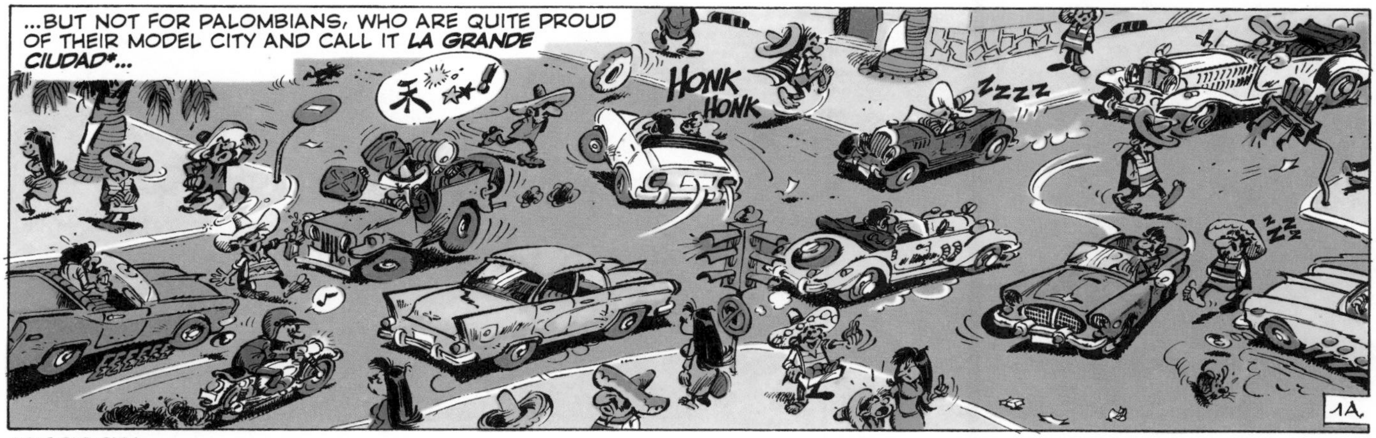
...BUT NOT FOR PALOMBIANS, WHO ARE QUITE PROUD OF THEIR MODEL CITY AND CALL IT ***LA GRANDE CIUDAD****...
HONK HONK
ZZZZ
1A.

*THE BIG CITY

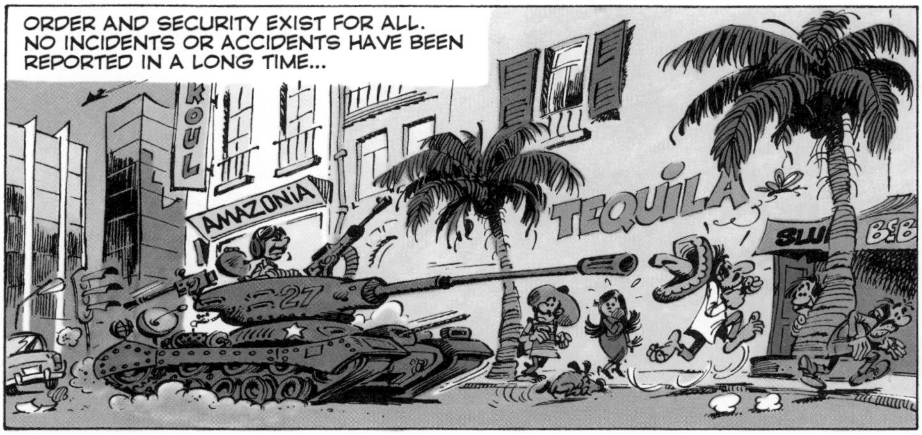
ORDER AND SECURITY EXIST FOR ALL. NO INCIDENTS OR ACCIDENTS HAVE BEEN REPORTED IN A LONG TIME...
AMAZONIA
TEQUILA

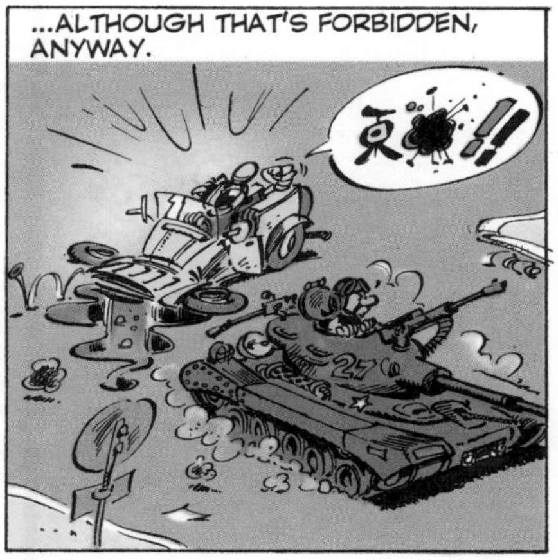
...ALTHOUGH THAT'S FORBIDDEN, ANYWAY.

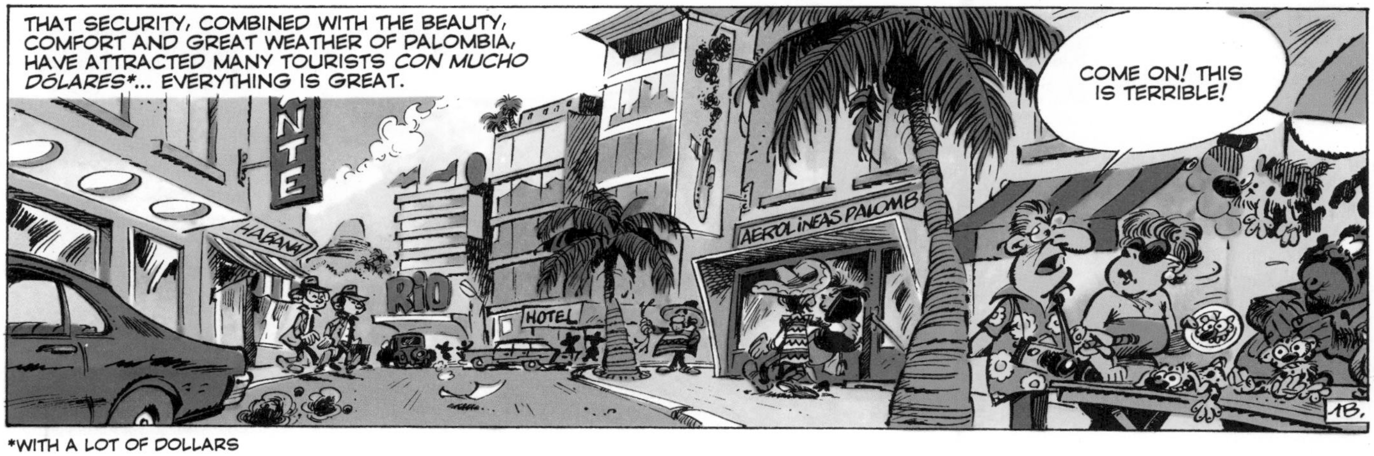
THAT SECURITY, COMBINED WITH THE BEAUTY, COMFORT AND GREAT WEATHER OF PALOMBIA, HAVE ATTRACTED MANY TOURISTS *CON MUCHO DÓLARES**... EVERYTHING IS GREAT.
COME ON! THIS IS TERRIBLE!
AEROLINEAS PALOMB
HOTEL
RIO
1B.

*WITH A LOT OF DOLLARS

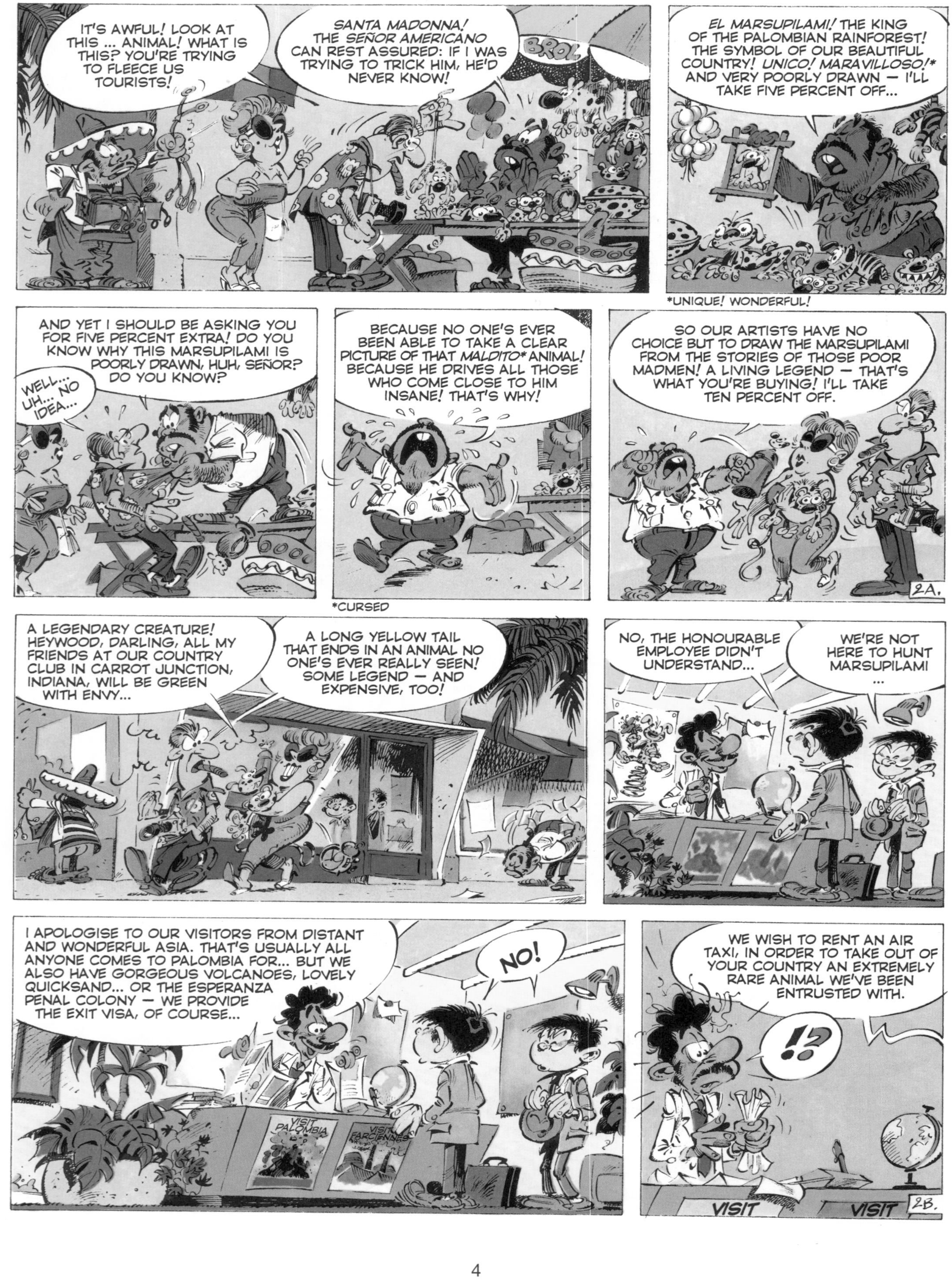
IT'S AWFUL! LOOK AT THIS ... ANIMAL! WHAT IS THIS? YOU'RE TRYING TO FLEECE US TOURISTS!
SANTA MADONNA! THE SEÑOR AMERICANO CAN REST ASSURED: IF I WAS TRYING TO TRICK HIM, HE'D NEVER KNOW!
BROL
EL MARSUPILAMI! THE KING OF THE PALOMBIAN RAINFOREST! THE SYMBOL OF OUR BEAUTIFUL COUNTRY! UNICO! MARAVILLOSO!* AND VERY POORLY DRAWN — I'LL TAKE FIVE PERCENT OFF...
*UNIQUE! WONDERFUL!
AND YET I SHOULD BE ASKING YOU FOR FIVE PERCENT EXTRA! DO YOU KNOW WHY THIS MARSUPILAMI IS POORLY DRAWN, HUH, SEÑOR? DO YOU KNOW?
WELL... UH... NO IDEA...
BECAUSE NO ONE'S EVER BEEN ABLE TO TAKE A CLEAR PICTURE OF THAT MALDITO* ANIMAL! BECAUSE HE DRIVES ALL THOSE WHO COME CLOSE TO HIM INSANE! THAT'S WHY!
*CURSED
SO OUR ARTISTS HAVE NO CHOICE BUT TO DRAW THE MARSUPILAMI FROM THE STORIES OF THOSE POOR MADMEN! A LIVING LEGEND — THAT'S WHAT YOU'RE BUYING! I'LL TAKE TEN PERCENT OFF.
2A.
A LEGENDARY CREATURE! HEYWOOD, DARLING, ALL MY FRIENDS AT OUR COUNTRY CLUB IN CARROT JUNCTION, INDIANA, WILL BE GREEN WITH ENVY...
A LONG YELLOW TAIL THAT ENDS IN AN ANIMAL NO ONE'S EVER REALLY SEEN! SOME LEGEND — AND EXPENSIVE, TOO!
NO, THE HONOURABLE EMPLOYEE DIDN'T UNDERSTAND...
WE'RE NOT HERE TO HUNT MARSUPILAMI ...
I APOLOGISE TO OUR VISITORS FROM DISTANT AND WONDERFUL ASIA. THAT'S USUALLY ALL ANYONE COMES TO PALOMBIA FOR... BUT WE ALSO HAVE GORGEOUS VOLCANOES, LOVELY QUICKSAND... OR THE ESPERANZA PENAL COLONY — WE PROVIDE THE EXIT VISA, OF COURSE...
NO!
VISIT PALOMBIA
VISIT
WE WISH TO RENT AN AIR TAXI, IN ORDER TO TAKE OUT OF YOUR COUNTRY AN EXTREMELY RARE ANIMAL WE'VE BEEN ENTRUSTED WITH.
!?
VISIT
VISIT
2B.

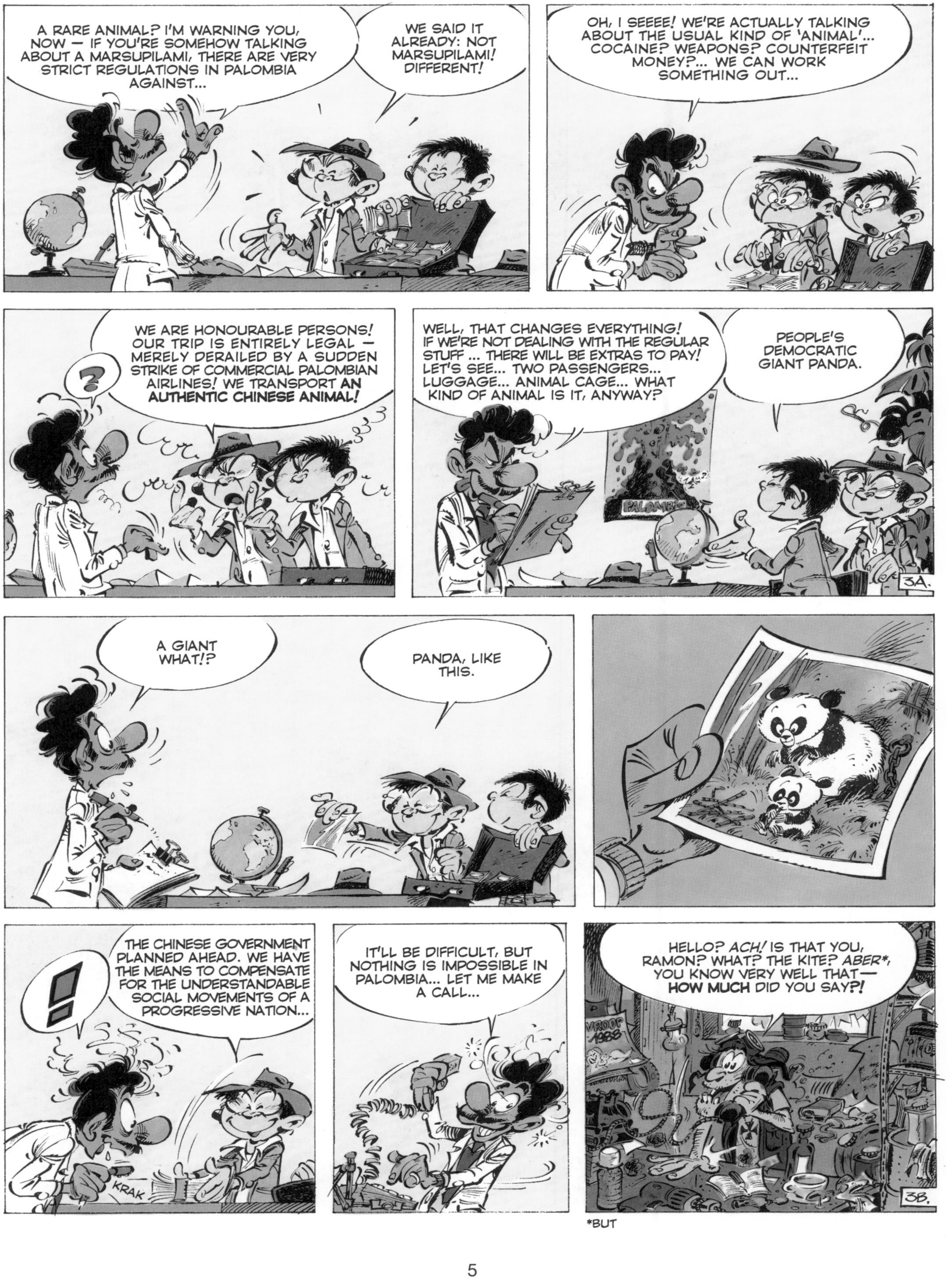
A RARE ANIMAL? I'M WARNING YOU, NOW — IF YOU'RE SOMEHOW TALKING ABOUT A MARSUPILAMI, THERE ARE VERY STRICT REGULATIONS IN PALOMBIA AGAINST...
WE SAID IT ALREADY: NOT MARSUPILAMI! DIFFERENT!
OH, I SEEEE! WE'RE ACTUALLY TALKING ABOUT THE USUAL KIND OF 'ANIMAL'... COCAINE? WEAPONS? COUNTERFEIT MONEY?... WE CAN WORK SOMETHING OUT...
?
WE ARE HONOURABLE PERSONS! OUR TRIP IS ENTIRELY LEGAL — MERELY DERAILED BY A SUDDEN STRIKE OF COMMERCIAL PALOMBIAN AIRLINES! WE TRANSPORT **AN AUTHENTIC CHINESE ANIMAL!**
WELL, THAT CHANGES EVERYTHING! IF WE'RE NOT DEALING WITH THE REGULAR STUFF ... THERE WILL BE EXTRAS TO PAY! LET'S SEE... TWO PASSENGERS... LUGGAGE... ANIMAL CAGE... WHAT KIND OF ANIMAL IS IT, ANYWAY?
PEOPLE'S DEMOCRATIC GIANT PANDA.
PALOMBIA
A GIANT WHAT!?
PANDA, LIKE THIS.
!
THE CHINESE GOVERNMENT PLANNED AHEAD. WE HAVE THE MEANS TO COMPENSATE FOR THE UNDERSTANDABLE SOCIAL MOVEMENTS OF A PROGRESSIVE NATION...
KRAK
IT'LL BE DIFFICULT, BUT NOTHING IS IMPOSSIBLE IN PALOMBIA... LET ME MAKE A CALL...
HELLO? *ACH!* IS THAT YOU, RAMON? WHAT? THE KITE? *ABER**, YOU KNOW VERY WELL THAT— **HOW MUCH** DID YOU SAY?!
VROOP 1988

*BUT

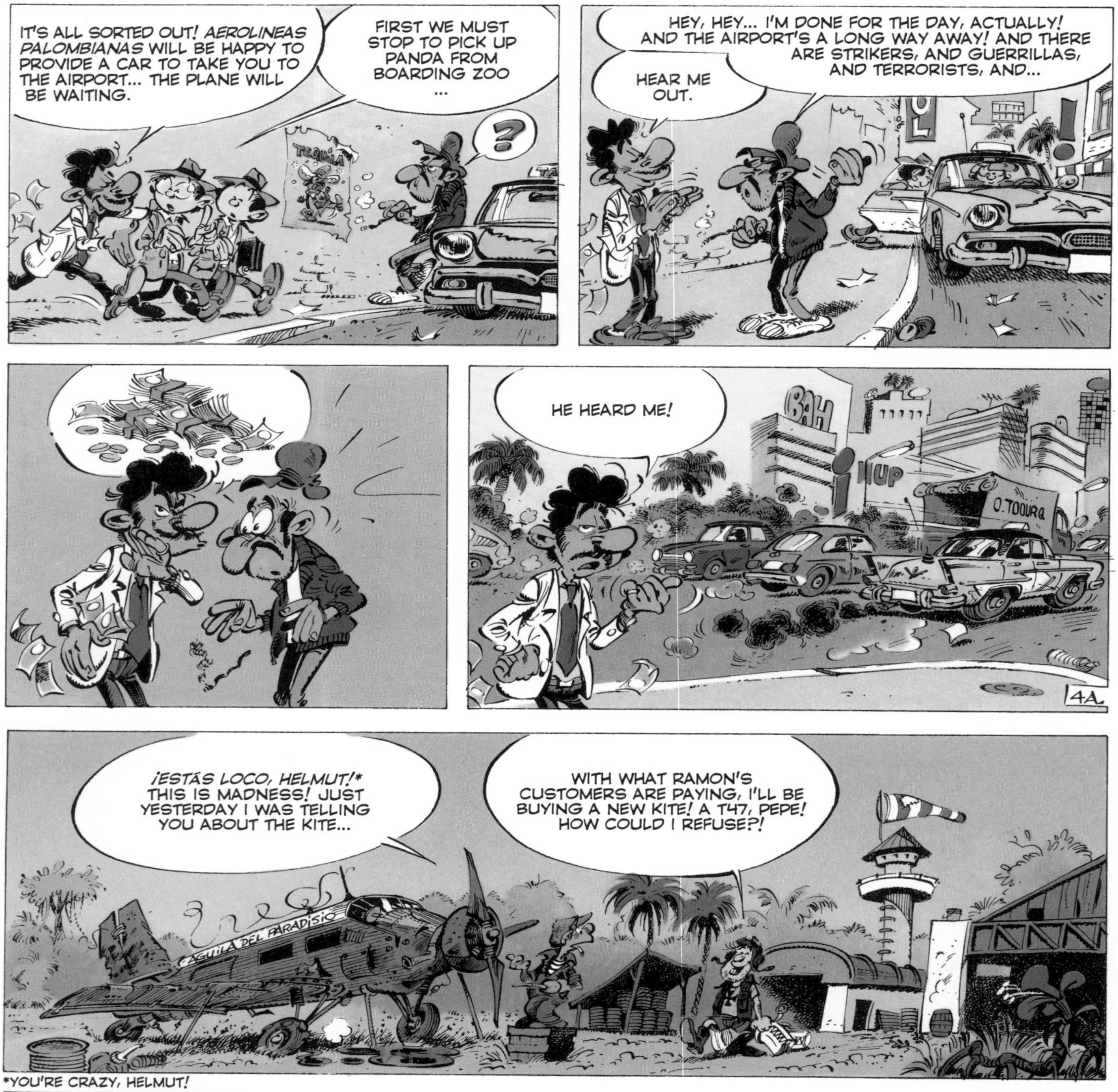
IT'S ALL SORTED OUT! *AEROLINEAS PALOMBIANAS* WILL BE HAPPY TO PROVIDE A CAR TO TAKE YOU TO THE AIRPORT... THE PLANE WILL BE WAITING.
FIRST WE MUST STOP TO PICK UP PANDA FROM BOARDING ZOO ...
TEQUILA
?
HEY, HEY... I'M DONE FOR THE DAY, ACTUALLY! AND THE AIRPORT'S A LONG WAY AWAY! AND THERE ARE STRIKERS, AND GUERRILLAS, AND TERRORISTS, AND...
HEAR ME OUT.
HE HEARD ME!
BAH
HUP
*¡ESTÁS LOCO, HELMUT!** THIS IS MADNESS! JUST YESTERDAY I WAS TELLING YOU ABOUT THE KITE...
WITH WHAT RAMON'S CUSTOMERS ARE PAYING, I'LL BE BUYING A NEW KITE! A T47, PEPE! HOW COULD I REFUSE?!
AGUILA DEL PARADISIO

*YOU'RE CRAZY, HELMUT!

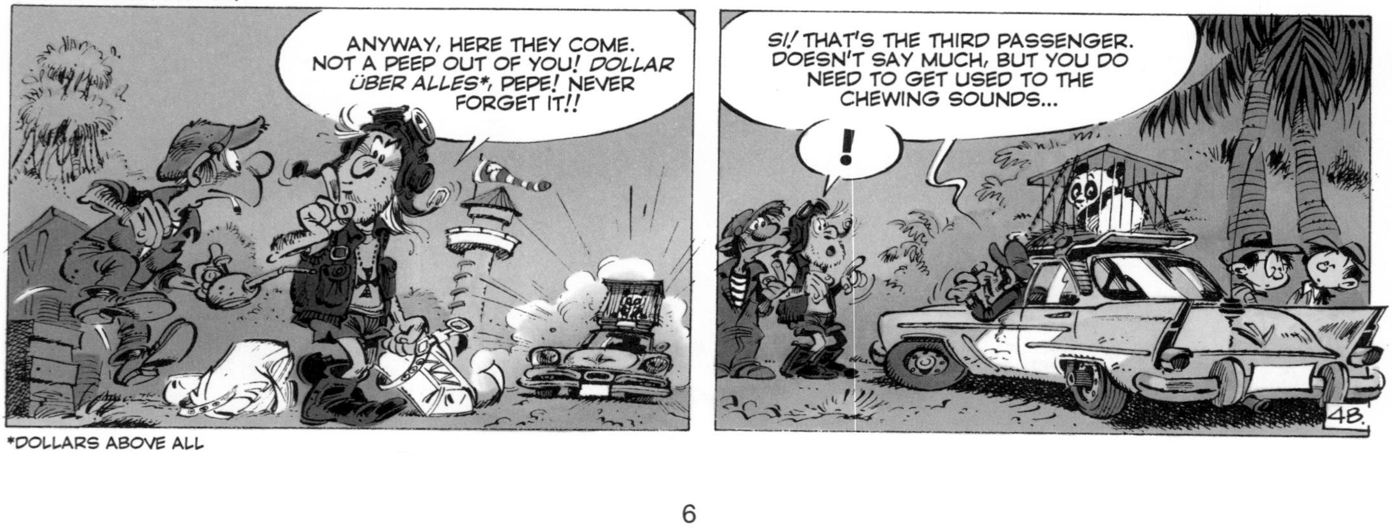
ANYWAY, HERE THEY COME. NOT A PEEP OUT OF YOU! *DOLLAR ÜBER ALLES**, PEPE! NEVER FORGET IT!!
SI! THAT'S THE THIRD PASSENGER. DOESN'T SAY MUCH, BUT YOU DO NEED TO GET USED TO THE CHEWING SOUNDS...
!

*DOLLARS ABOVE ALL

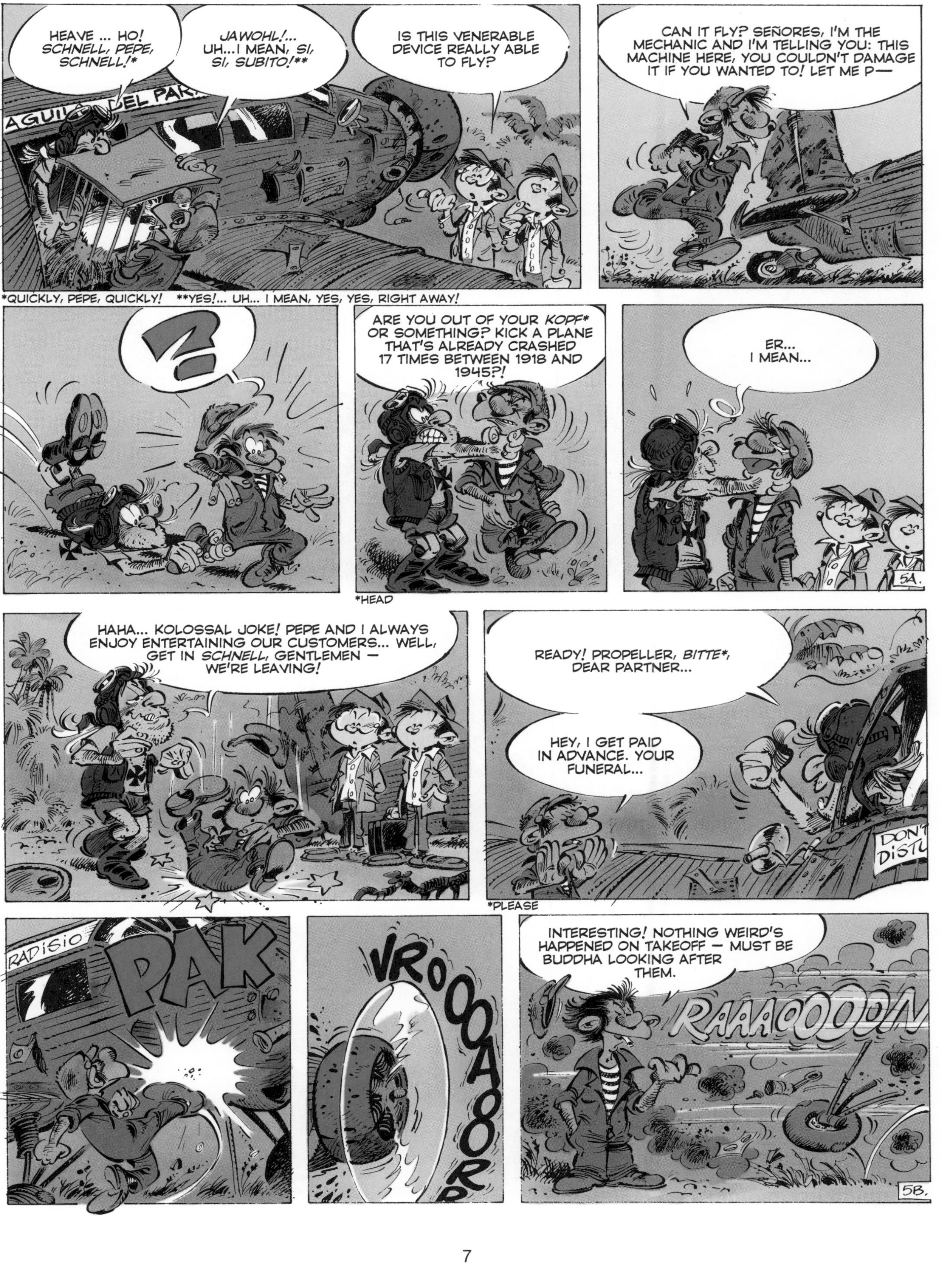

HEAVE ... HO! SCHNELL, PEPE, SCHNELL!*
JAWOHL!... UH...I MEAN, SI, SI, SUBITO!**
AGUILA DEL PAR
IS THIS VENERABLE DEVICE REALLY ABLE TO FLY?
CAN IT FLY? SEÑORES, I'M THE MECHANIC AND I'M TELLING YOU: THIS MACHINE HERE, YOU COULDN'T DAMAGE IT IF YOU WANTED TO! LET ME P—
*QUICKLY, PEPE, QUICKLY! **YES!... UH... I MEAN, YES, YES, RIGHT AWAY!
?
ARE YOU OUT OF YOUR KOPF* OR SOMETHING? KICK A PLANE THAT'S ALREADY CRASHED 17 TIMES BETWEEN 1918 AND 1945?!
*HEAD
ER... I MEAN...
5A.
HAHA... KOLOSSAL JOKE! PEPE AND I ALWAYS ENJOY ENTERTAINING OUR CUSTOMERS... WELL, GET IN SCHNELL, GENTLEMEN — WE'RE LEAVING!
READY! PROPELLER, BITTE*, DEAR PARTNER...
HEY, I GET PAID IN ADVANCE. YOUR FUNERAL...
DON'T DISTU
*PLEASE
RADISIO
PAK
VROOOOAOOORR
INTERESTING! NOTHING WEIRD'S HAPPENED ON TAKEOFF — MUST BE BUDDHA LOOKING AFTER THEM.
RAAAOOOON
5B.

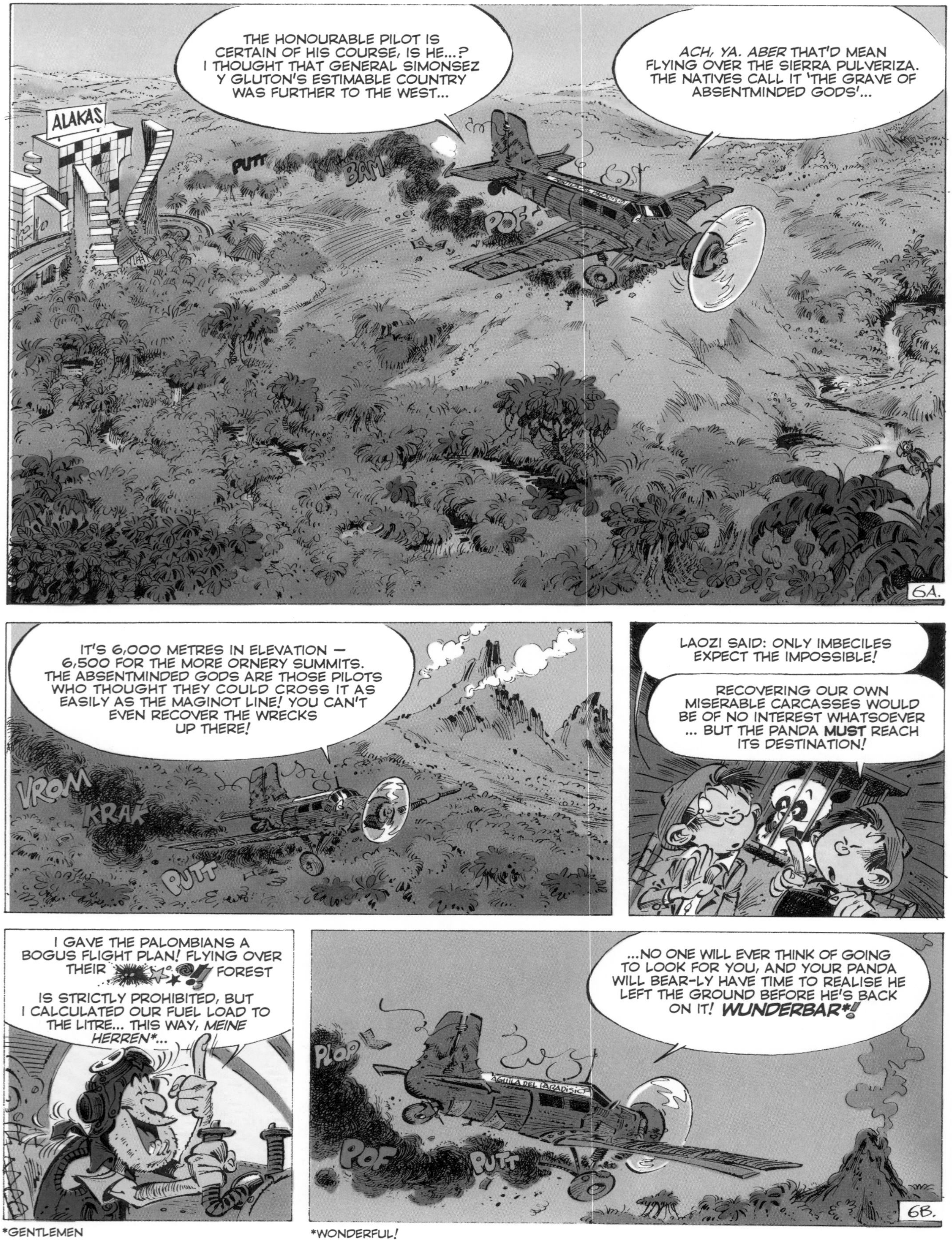
ALAKAS
THE HONOURABLE PILOT IS CERTAIN OF HIS COURSE, IS HE...? I THOUGHT THAT GENERAL SIMONSEZ Y GLUTON'S ESTIMABLE COUNTRY WAS FURTHER TO THE WEST...
ACH, YA. ABER THAT'D MEAN FLYING OVER THE SIERRA PULVERIZA. THE NATIVES CALL IT 'THE GRAVE OF ABSENTMINDED GODS'...
PUTT
BAM
POF
6A.
IT'S 6,000 METRES IN ELEVATION — 6,500 FOR THE MORE ORNERY SUMMITS. THE ABSENTMINDED GODS ARE THOSE PILOTS WHO THOUGHT THEY COULD CROSS IT AS EASILY AS THE MAGINOT LINE! YOU CAN'T EVEN RECOVER THE WRECKS UP THERE!
VROM
KRAK
PUTT
LAOZI SAID: ONLY IMBECILES EXPECT THE IMPOSSIBLE!
RECOVERING OUR OWN MISERABLE CARCASSES WOULD BE OF NO INTEREST WHATSOEVER ... BUT THE PANDA **MUST** REACH ITS DESTINATION!
I GAVE THE PALOMBIANS A BOGUS FLIGHT PLAN! FLYING OVER THEIR FOREST IS STRICTLY PROHIBITED, BUT I CALCULATED OUR FUEL LOAD TO THE LITRE... THIS WAY, *MEINE HERREN**...
...NO ONE WILL EVER THINK OF GOING TO LOOK FOR YOU, AND YOUR PANDA WILL BEAR-LY HAVE TIME TO REALISE HE LEFT THE GROUND BEFORE HE'S BACK ON IT! ***WUNDERBAR**!***
PLOP
AGUILA DEL PARADISIO
POF
PUTT
6B.

*GENTLEMEN

*WONDERFUL!

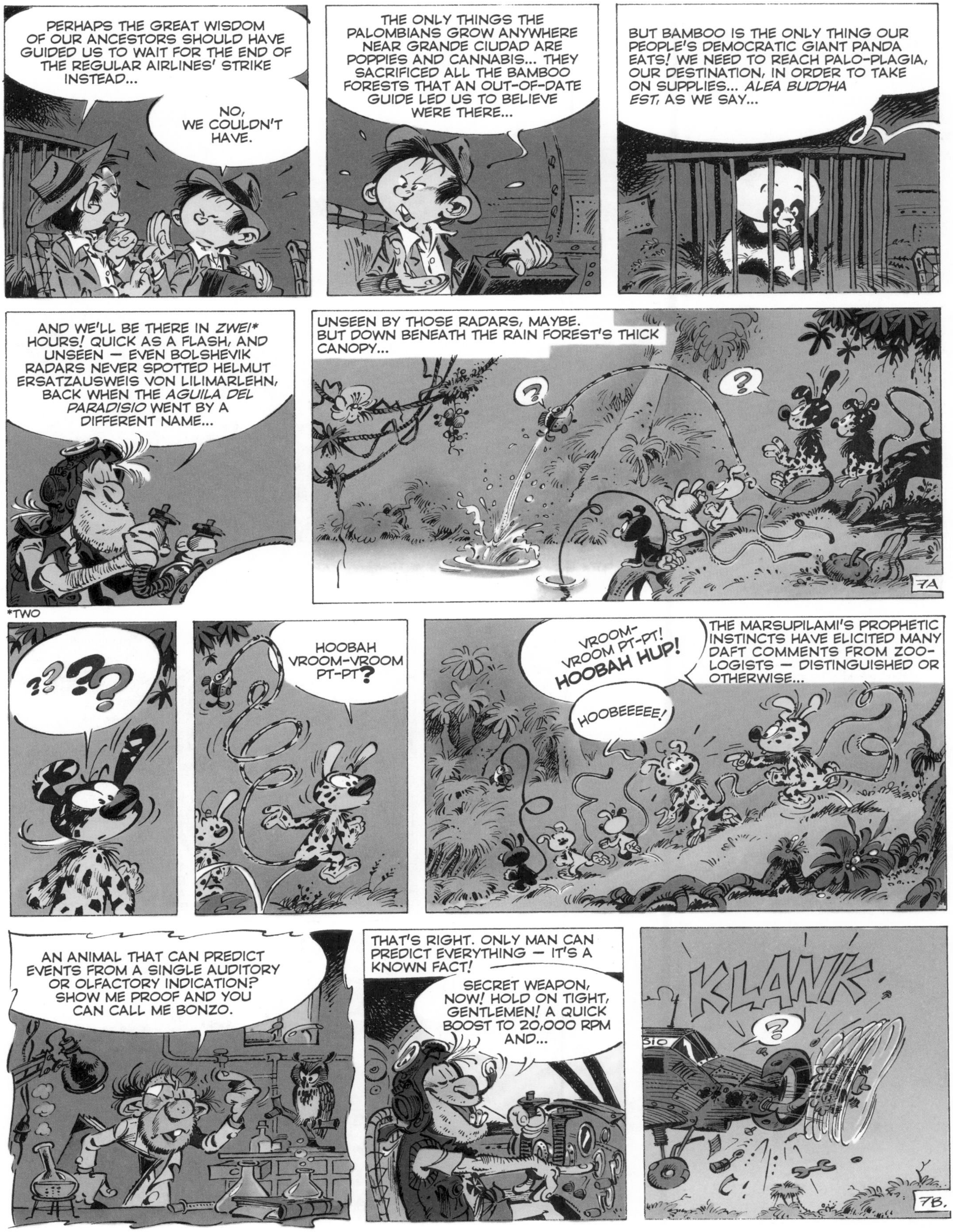
PERHAPS THE GREAT WISDOM OF OUR ANCESTORS SHOULD HAVE GUIDED US TO WAIT FOR THE END OF THE REGULAR AIRLINES' STRIKE INSTEAD...
NO, WE COULDN'T HAVE.
THE ONLY THINGS THE PALOMBIANS GROW ANYWHERE NEAR GRANDE CIUDAD ARE POPPIES AND CANNABIS... THEY SACRIFICED ALL THE BAMBOO FORESTS THAT AN OUT-OF-DATE GUIDE LED US TO BELIEVE WERE THERE...
BUT BAMBOO IS THE ONLY THING OUR PEOPLE'S DEMOCRATIC GIANT PANDA EATS! WE NEED TO REACH PALO-PLAGIA, OUR DESTINATION, IN ORDER TO TAKE ON SUPPLIES... *ALEA BUDDHA EST*, AS WE SAY...
AND WE'LL BE THERE IN *ZWEI!** HOURS! QUICK AS A FLASH, AND UNSEEN — EVEN BOLSHEVIK RADARS NEVER SPOTTED HELMUT ERSATZAUSWEIS VON LILIMARLEHN, BACK WHEN THE *AGUILA DEL PARADISIO* WENT BY A DIFFERENT NAME...
UNSEEN BY THOSE RADARS, MAYBE. BUT DOWN BENEATH THE RAIN FOREST'S THICK CANOPY...
?
?
7A
?? ??
HOOBAH VROOM-VROOM PT-PT?
VROOM-VROOM PT-PT! HOOBAH HUP!
THE MARSUPILAMI'S PROPHETIC INSTINCTS HAVE ELICITED MANY DAFT COMMENTS FROM ZOO-LOGISTS — DISTINGUISHED OR OTHERWISE...
HOOBEEEEEE!
AN ANIMAL THAT CAN PREDICT EVENTS FROM A SINGLE AUDITORY OR OLFACTORY INDICATION? SHOW ME PROOF AND YOU CAN CALL ME BONZO.
THAT'S RIGHT. ONLY MAN CAN PREDICT EVERYTHING — IT'S A KNOWN FACT!
SECRET WEAPON, NOW! HOLD ON TIGHT, GENTLEMEN! A QUICK BOOST TO 20,000 RPM AND...
KLANK
?
7B.

*TWO

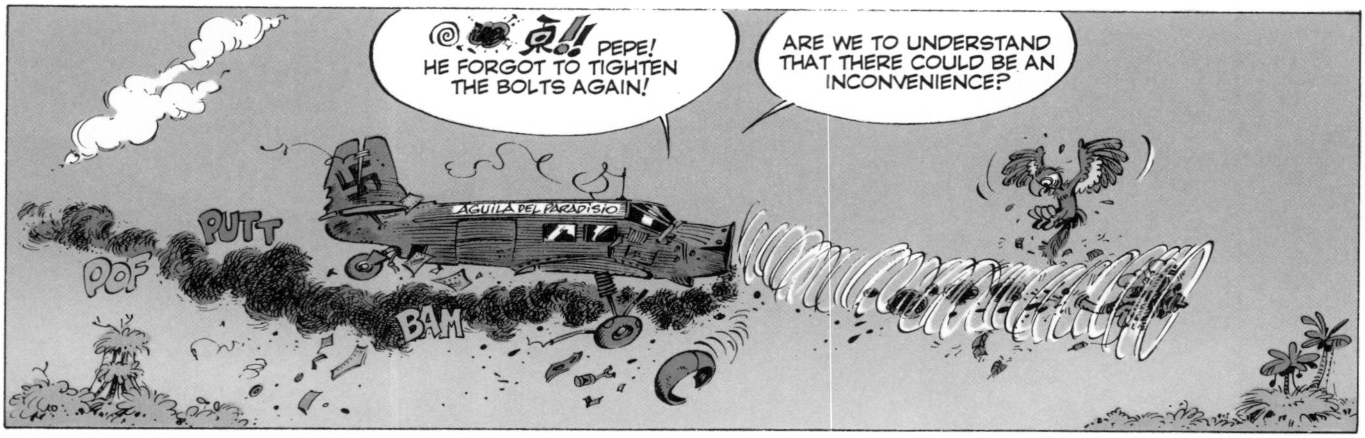
PEPE! HE FORGOT TO TIGHTEN THE BOLTS AGAIN!
ARE WE TO UNDERSTAND THAT THERE COULD BE AN INCONVENIENCE?
AGUILA DEL PARADISIO
PUTT
POF
BAM

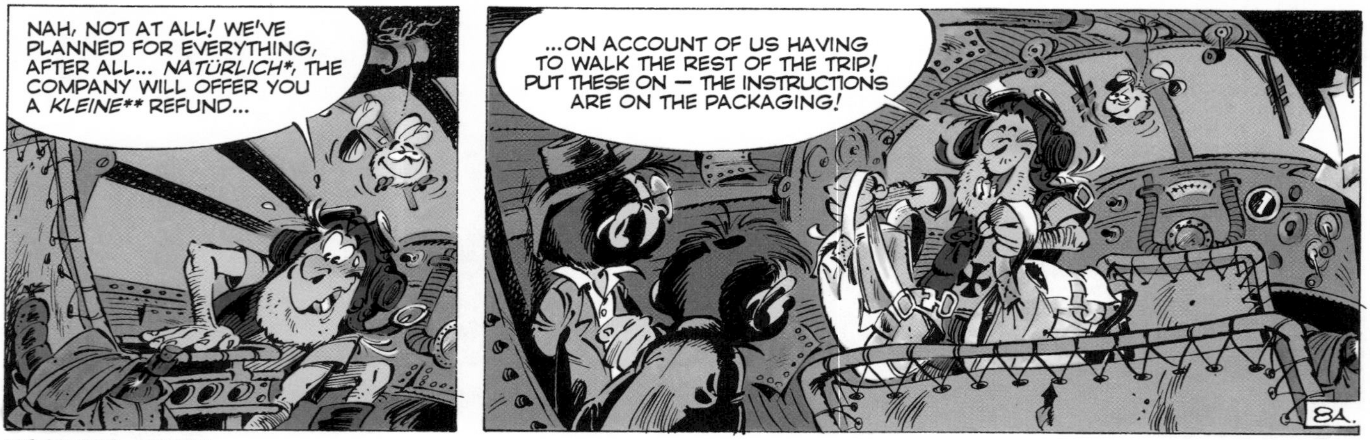
NAH, NOT AT ALL! WE'VE PLANNED FOR EVERYTHING, AFTER ALL... *NATÜRLICH**, THE COMPANY WILL OFFER YOU A *KLEINE*** REFUND...
...ON ACCOUNT OF US HAVING TO WALK THE REST OF THE TRIP! PUT THESE ON — THE INSTRUCTIONS ARE ON THE PACKAGING!

*OF COURSE **SMALL

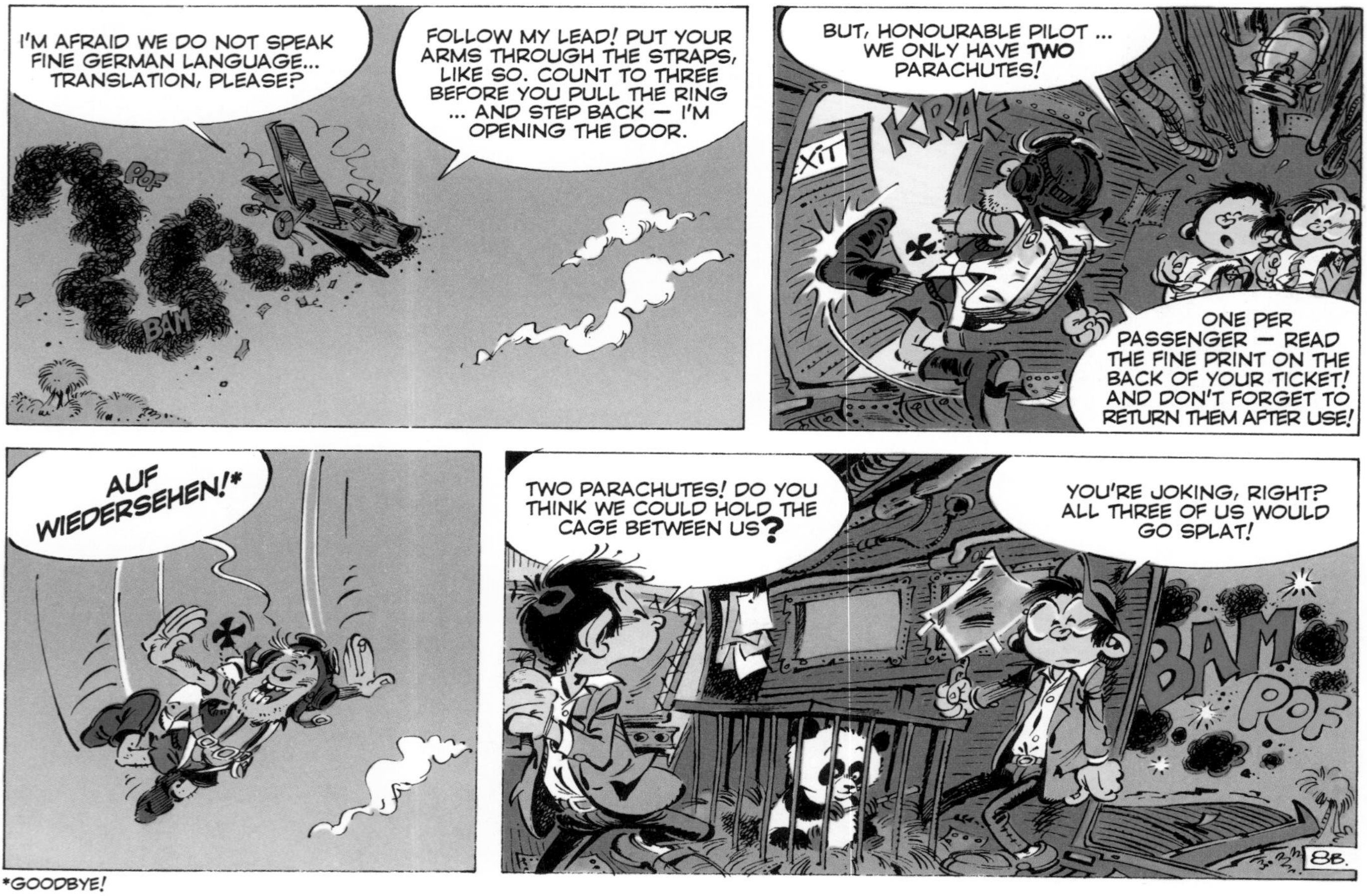
I'M AFRAID WE DO NOT SPEAK FINE GERMAN LANGUAGE... TRANSLATION, PLEASE?
FOLLOW MY LEAD! PUT YOUR ARMS THROUGH THE STRAPS, LIKE SO. COUNT TO THREE BEFORE YOU PULL THE RING ... AND STEP BACK — I'M OPENING THE DOOR.
POF
BAM
BUT, HONOURABLE PILOT ... WE ONLY HAVE **TWO** PARACHUTES!
EXIT
KRAK
ONE PER PASSENGER — READ THE FINE PRINT ON THE BACK OF YOUR TICKET! AND DON'T FORGET TO RETURN THEM AFTER USE!
AUF WIEDERSEHEN!*
TWO PARACHUTES! DO YOU THINK WE COULD HOLD THE CAGE BETWEEN US?
YOU'RE JOKING, RIGHT? ALL THREE OF US WOULD GO SPLAT!
BAM
POF

*GOODBYE!

KRAK BAM BOM PUTT

THE GREAT FRENCH MANDARIN MARCEL PAGNOL SAID IT BEST: 'HONOUR IS LIKE A MATCH — YOU CAN ONLY USE IT ONCE' ...

HE WAS ABSOLUTELY CORRECT! OUCH!

FLOP PUTT

MAY THE DEMOCRATIC GODS LOOK AFTER OUR HONOURABLE REPUBLIC'S PANDA AND OFFER IT OUR APOLOGIES!

POF PAF KRAK

NOM SLURP GULP!

9A.

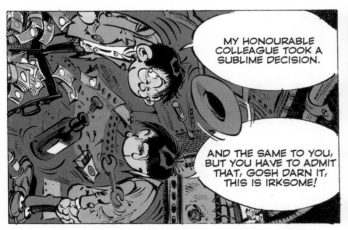

MY HONOURABLE COLLEAGUE TOOK A SUBLIME DECISION.

AND THE SAME TO YOU, BUT YOU HAVE TO ADMIT THAT, GOSH DARN IT, THIS IS IRKSOME!

POP VROP ROP VROOM RRR

?!

FWOOM

?

?

?

WHEN WE CLAIMED THAT THE MARSUPILAMI HAD PROPHETIC INSTINCTS, WE DIDN'T MEAN HE HAD AN EXCLUSIVE. OTHER BIZARRE MAMMALS MERELY NEED THE ALARMING SOUND TO BE A TAD LOUDER, THAT'S ALL...

FWOOM? WAH WASSAT?

?

?

?

9B.

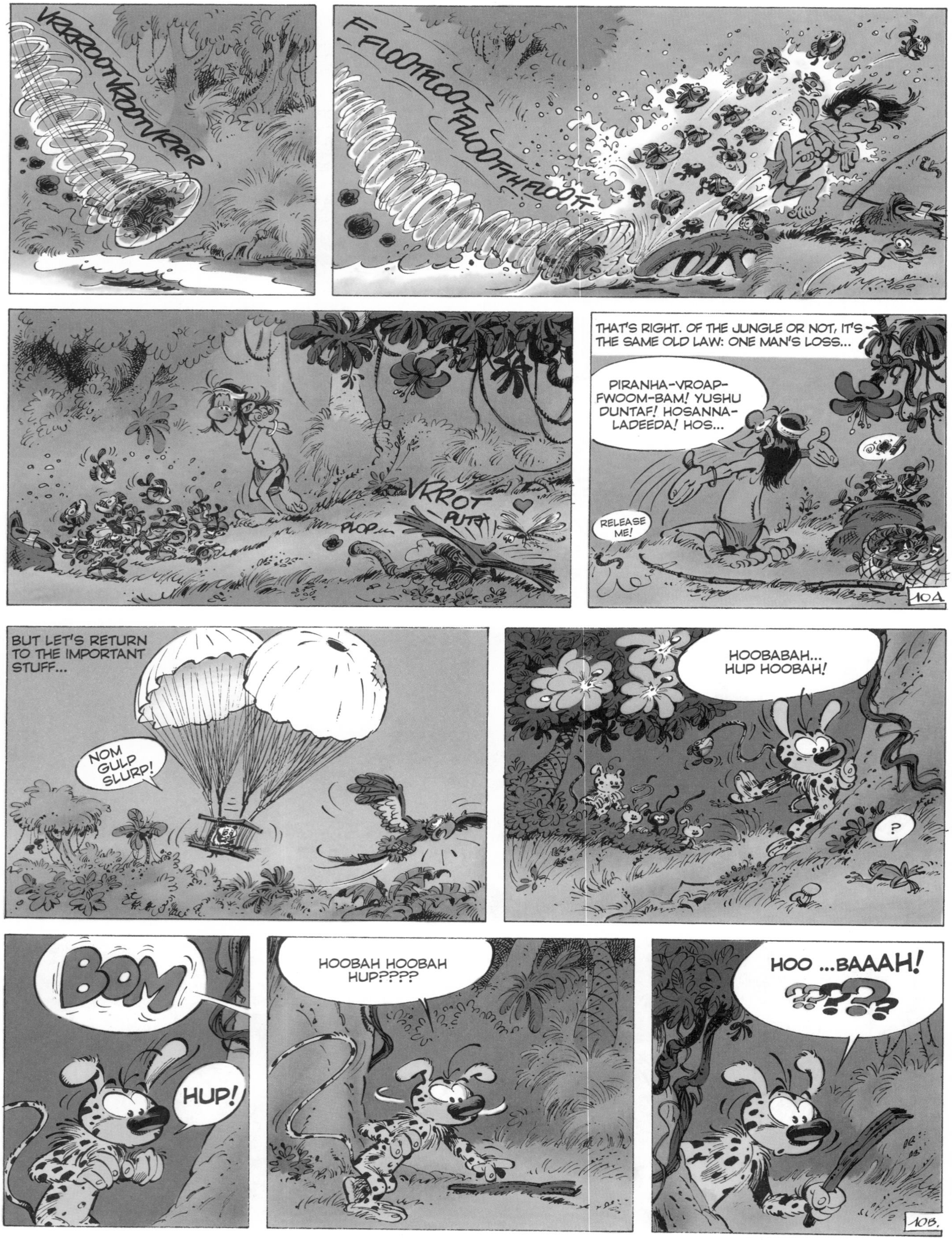
VRRROOTVROOTVRRR
FFLOOTFLOOTFLOOTFLOOTTHFLOOTT
VRROT
PUTT
PLOP
THAT'S RIGHT. OF THE JUNGLE OR NOT, IT'S THE SAME OLD LAW: ONE MAN'S LOSS...
PIRANHA-VROAP-FWOOM-BAM! YUSHU DUNTAF! HOSANNA-LADEEDA! HOS...
RELEASE ME!
BUT LET'S RETURN TO THE IMPORTANT STUFF...
NOM GULP SLURP!
HOOBABAH... HUP HOOBAH!
?
BOM
HUP!
HOOBAH HOOBAH HUP????
HOO ...BAAAH!
???????

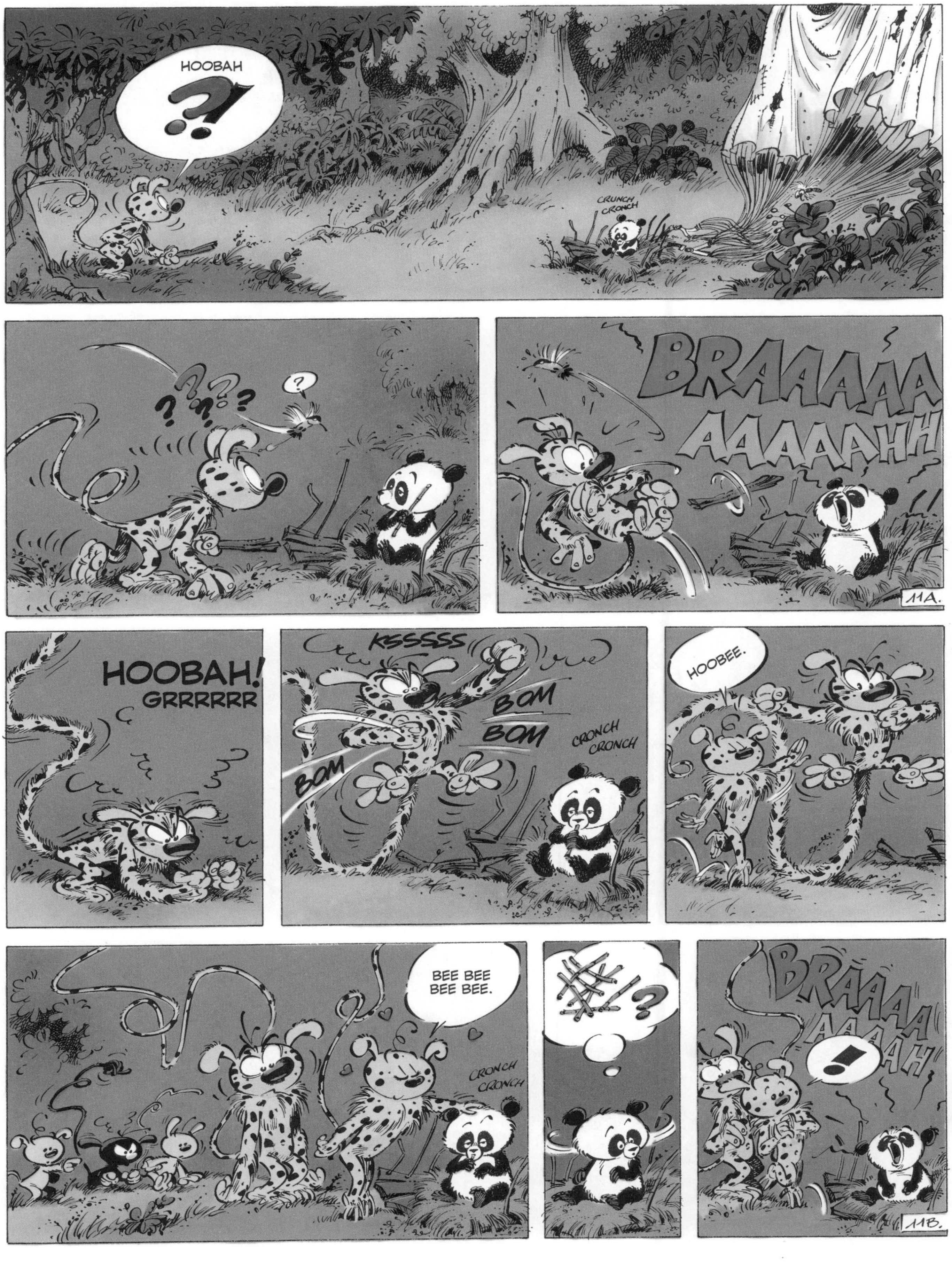
HOOBAH
CRUNCH CRONCH
BRAAAAAAAAAAAHH
11A.
HOOBAH! GRRRRRR
KSSSSS
BOM BOM BOM
CRONCH CRONCH
HOOBEE.
BEE BEE BEE BEE.
CRONCH CRONCH
BRAAAAAAAAAH
11B.

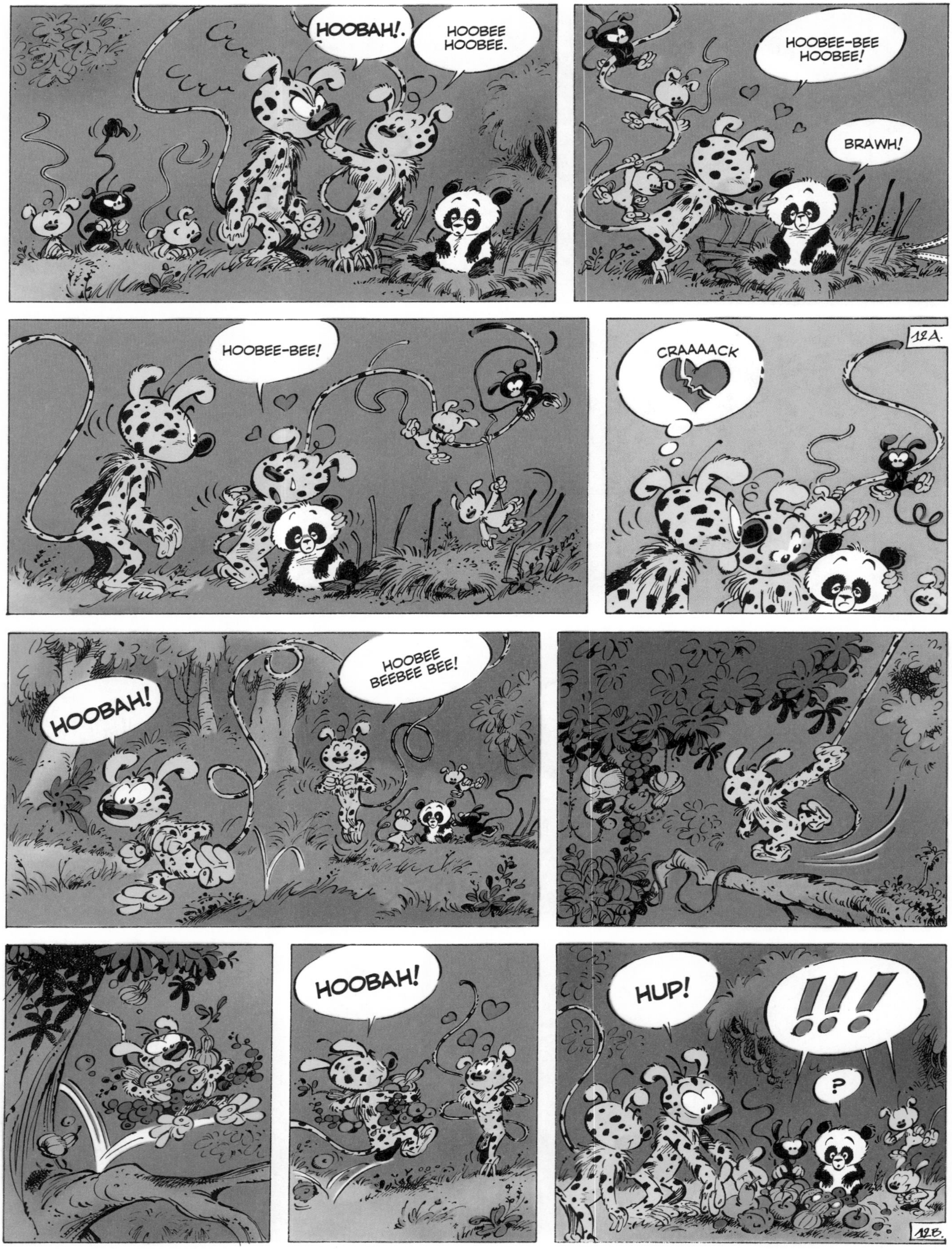
HOOBAH!.
HOOBEE HOOBEE.
HOOBEE-BEE HOOBEE!
BRAWH!
HOOBEE-BEE!
CRAAAACK
12A.
HOOBAH!
HOOBEE BEEBEE BEE!
HOOBAH!
HUP!
!!!
?
12B.

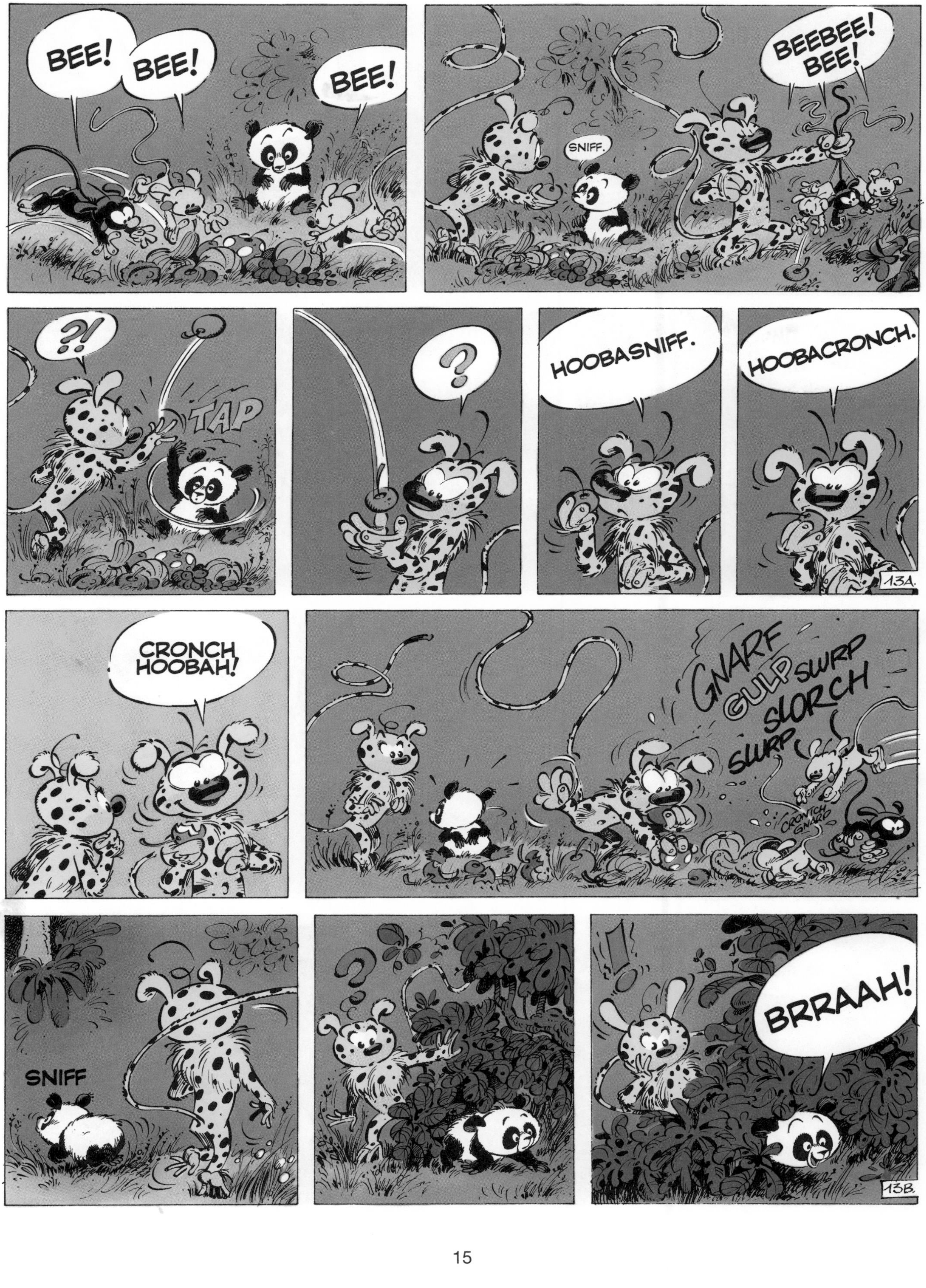
BEE!
BEE!
BEE!
BEEBEE! BEE!
SNIFF.
?!
TAP
?
HOOBASNIFF.
HOOBACRONCH.
13A.
CRONCH HOOBAH!
GNARF
GULP
SWRP
SLORCH
SLURP
CRONTCH GNARD
SNIFF
?
!
BRRAAH!
13B.

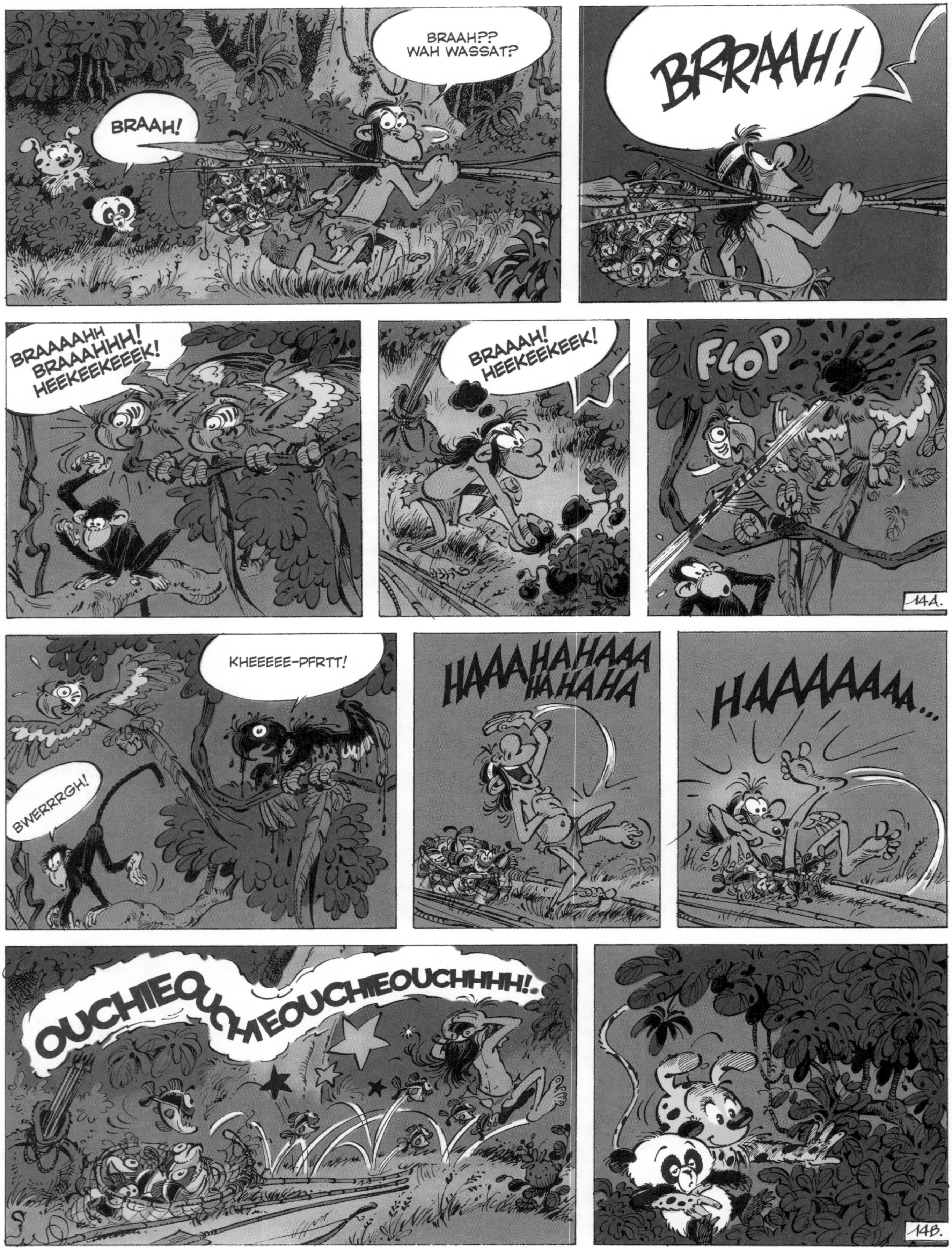
BRAAH!
BRAAH?? WAH WASSAT?
BRRAAH!
BRAAAAHH BRAAAHHH! HEEKEEKEEEK!
BRAAAH! HEEKEEKEEK!
FLOP
14A.
KHEEEEE-PFRTT!
BWERRRGH!
HAAAHAHAAA HAHAHA
HAAAAAAA...
OUCHIEOUCHIEOUCHIEOUCHHHH!
14B.

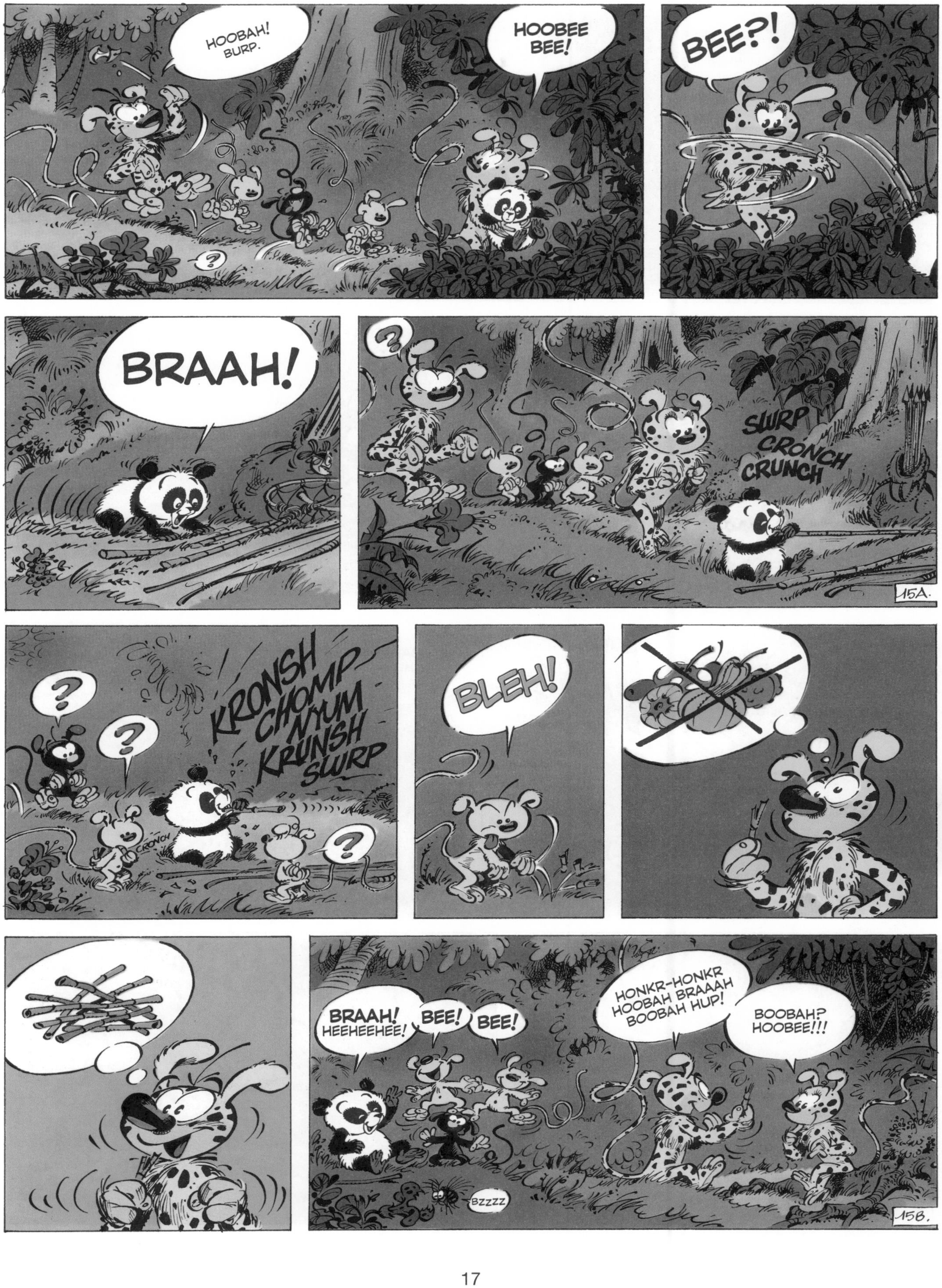
HOOBAH! BURP.
HOOBEE BEE!
BEE?!
BRAAH!
SLURP CRONCH CRUNCH
15A.
KRONSH CHOMP NYUM KRUNSH SLURP
CRONCH
BLEH!
BRAAH! HEEHEEHEE!
BEE!
BEE!
HONKR-HONKR HOOBAH BRAAAH BOOBAH HUP!
BOOBAH? HOOBEE!!!
BZZZZ
15B.

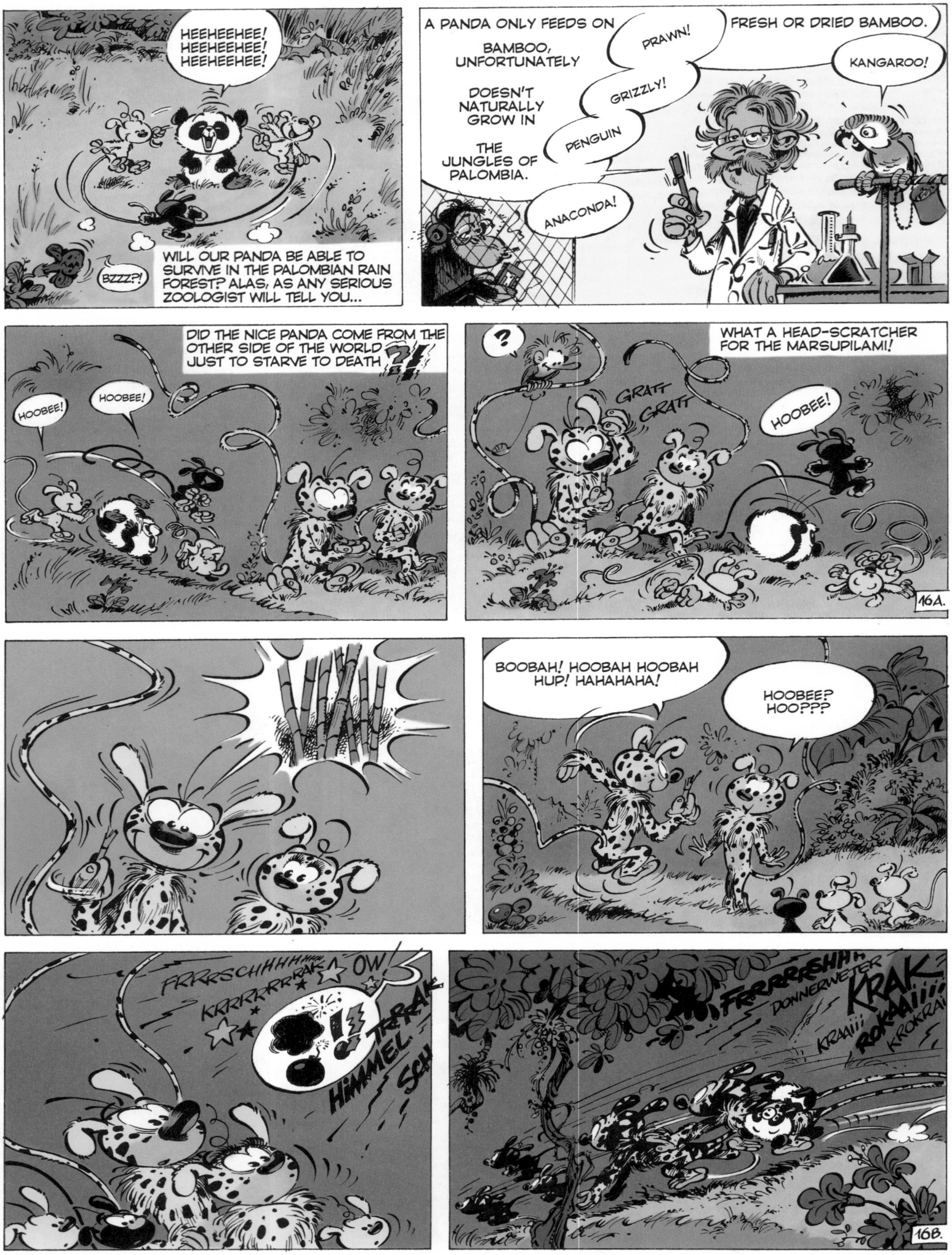
HEEHEEHEE! HEEHEEHEE! HEEHEEHEE!
BZZZ?!
WILL OUR PANDA BE ABLE TO SURVIVE IN THE PALOMBIAN RAIN FOREST? ALAS, AS ANY SERIOUS ZOOLOGIST WILL TELL YOU...
A PANDA ONLY FEEDS ON
PRAWN!
FRESH OR DRIED BAMBOO.
KANGAROO!
BAMBOO, UNFORTUNATELY
GRIZZLY!
DOESN'T NATURALLY GROW IN
PENGUIN
THE JUNGLES OF PALOMBIA.
ANACONDA!
DID THE NICE PANDA COME FROM THE OTHER SIDE OF THE WORLD JUST TO STARVE TO DEATH ?!
HOOBEE!
HOOBEE!
WHAT A HEAD-SCRATCHER FOR THE MARSUPILAMI!
?
GRATT GRATT
HOOBEE!
16A.
BOOBAH! HOOBAH HOOBAH HUP! HAHAHAHA!
HOOBEE? HOO???
FRRRSCHHHH
KRRRRRRAK
OW!
TRRRAK
HIMMEL
SCH
FRRRRRSHH
DONNERWETTER
KRAK
KRAAiii
ROKAA
KROKRA
16B.

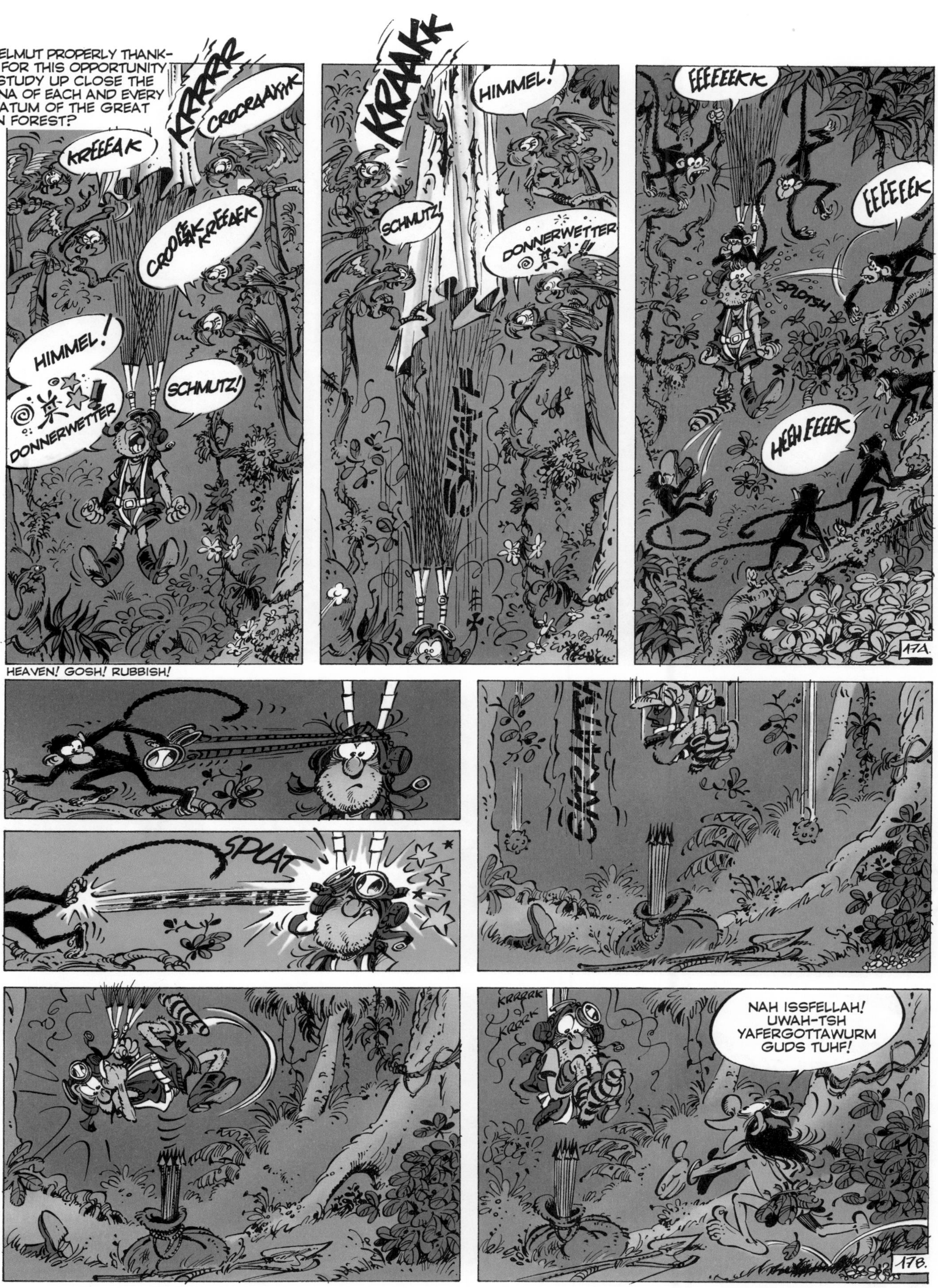

IS HELMUT PROPERLY THANKFUL FOR THIS OPPORTUNITY TO STUDY UP CLOSE THE FAUNA OF EACH AND EVERY STRATUM OF THE GREAT RAIN FOREST?
KRRRR
CROORAAKK
KREEEAK
CROOEEAK KREEAEK
HIMMEL!
DONNERWETTER
SCHMUTZ!
KRAAKK
HIMMEL!
SCHMUTZ!
DONNERWETTER
EEEEEEKK
EEEEEEK
SPLOTSH
HEEHEEEEK
17A.
HEAVEN! GOSH! RUBBISH!
SPLAT
KRRRRK
KRRRK
NAH ISSFELLAH! UWAH-TSH YAFERGOTTAWURM GUDS TUHF!
17B.

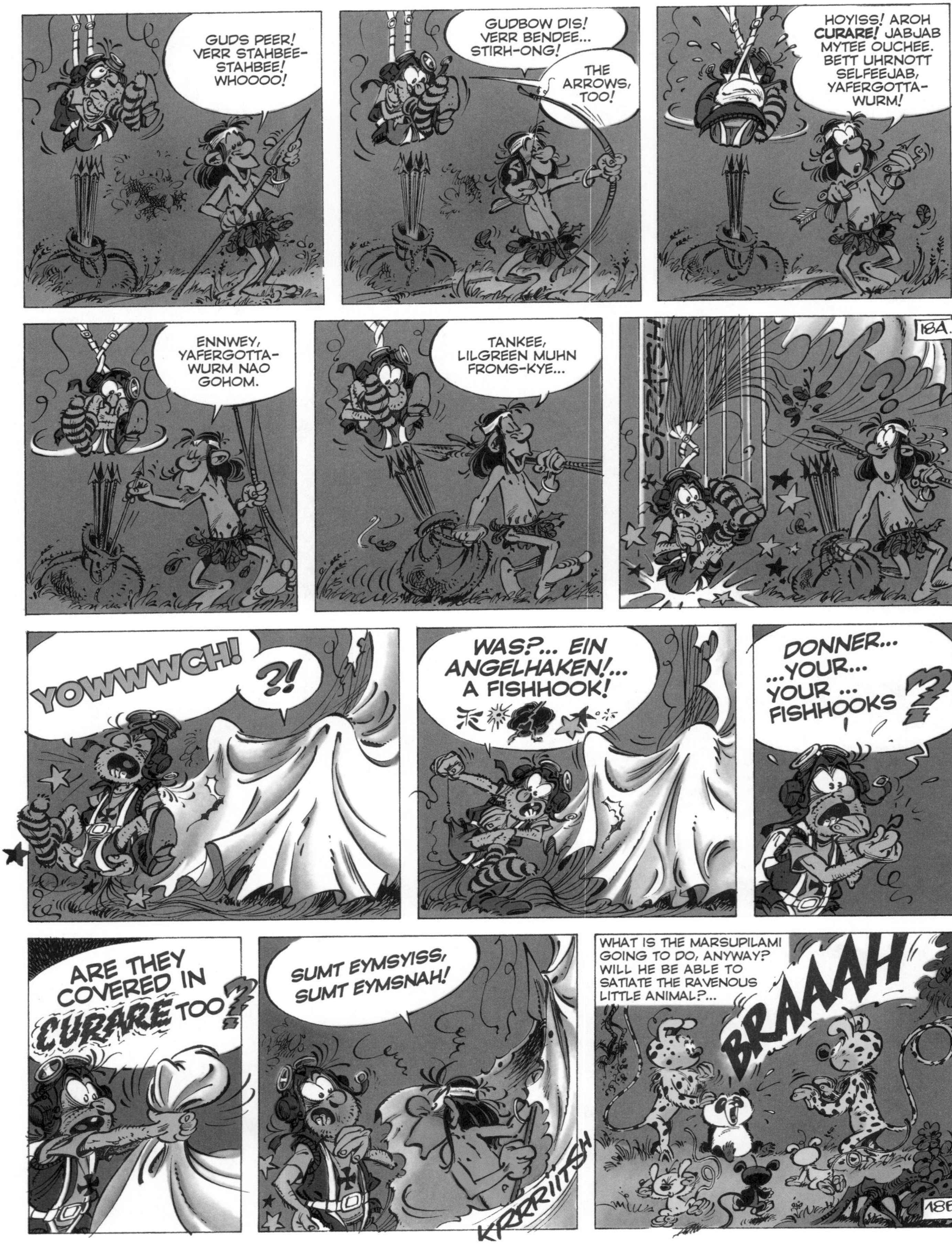

GUDS PEER! VERR STAHBEE-STAHBEE! WHOOOO!
GUDBOW DIS! VERR BENDEE... STIRH-ONG!
THE ARROWS, TOO!
HOYISS! AROH CURARE! JABJAB MYTEE OUCHEE. BETT UHRNOTT SELFEEJAB, YAFERGOTTA-WURM!
ENNWEY, YAFERGOTTA-WURM NAO GOHOM.
TANKEE, LILGREEN MUHN FROMS-KYE...
18A.
SPLATSH
YOWWWCH!
?!
WAS?... EIN ANGELHAKEN!... A FISHHOOK!
DONNER... ...YOUR... YOUR ... FISHHOOKS?
ARE THEY COVERED IN CURARE TOO?
SUMT EYMSYISS, SUMT EYMSNAH!
KRRRIITSH
WHAT IS THE MARSUPILAMI GOING TO DO, ANYWAY? WILL HE BE ABLE TO SATIATE THE RAVENOUS LITTLE ANIMAL?...
BRAAAH
18B

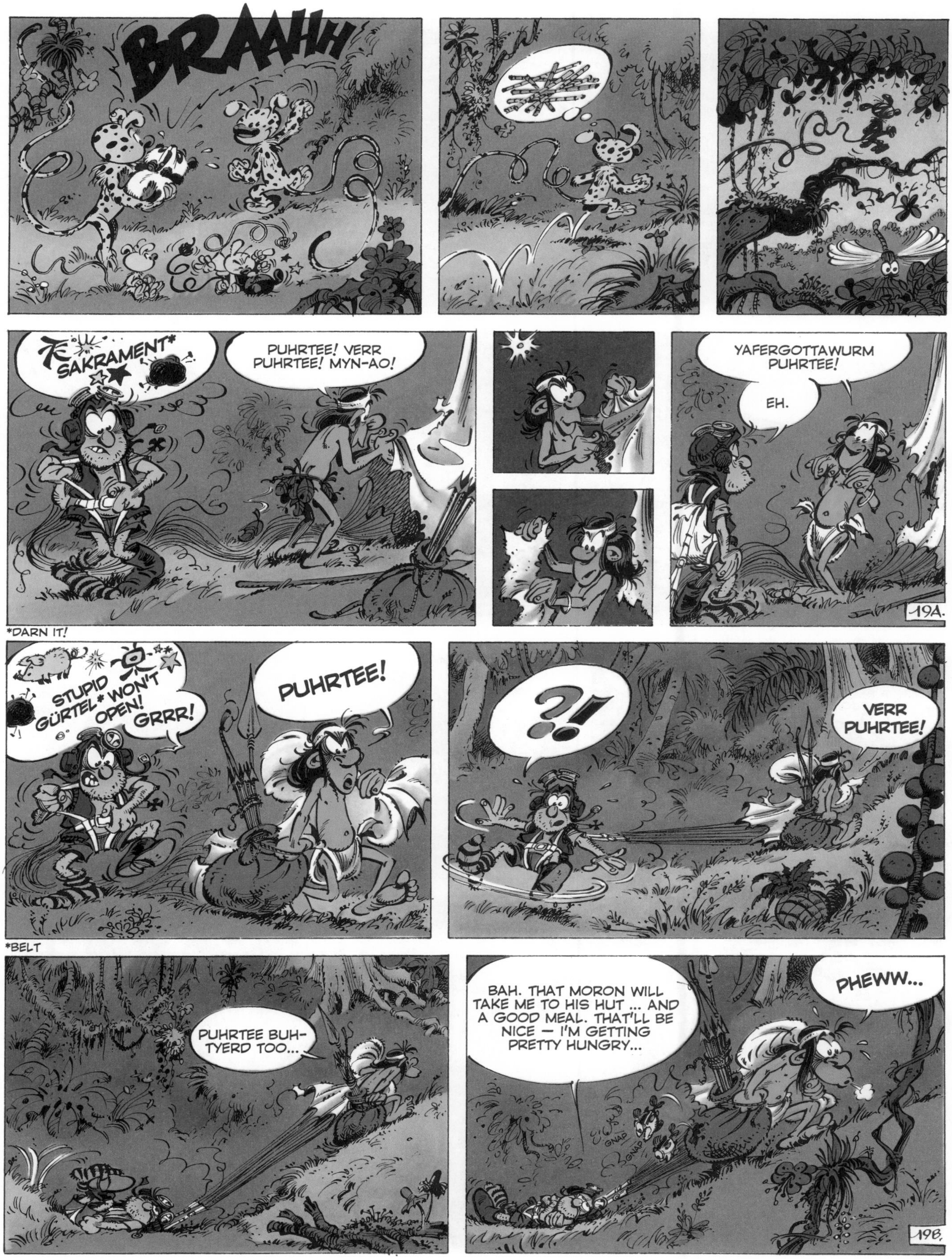
BRAAHH
SAKRAMENT*
PUHRTEE! VERR PUHRTEE! MYN-AO!
YAFERGOTTAWURM PUHRTEE!
EH.
19A.
*DARN IT!
STUPID GÜRTEL* WON'T OPEN! GRRR!
PUHRTEE!
?!
VERR PUHRTEE!
*BELT
PUHRTEE BUH-TYERD TOO...
BAH. THAT MORON WILL TAKE ME TO HIS HUT ... AND A GOOD MEAL. THAT'LL BE NICE — I'M GETTING PRETTY HUNGRY...
PHEWW...
GNAP
GNAP
19B.

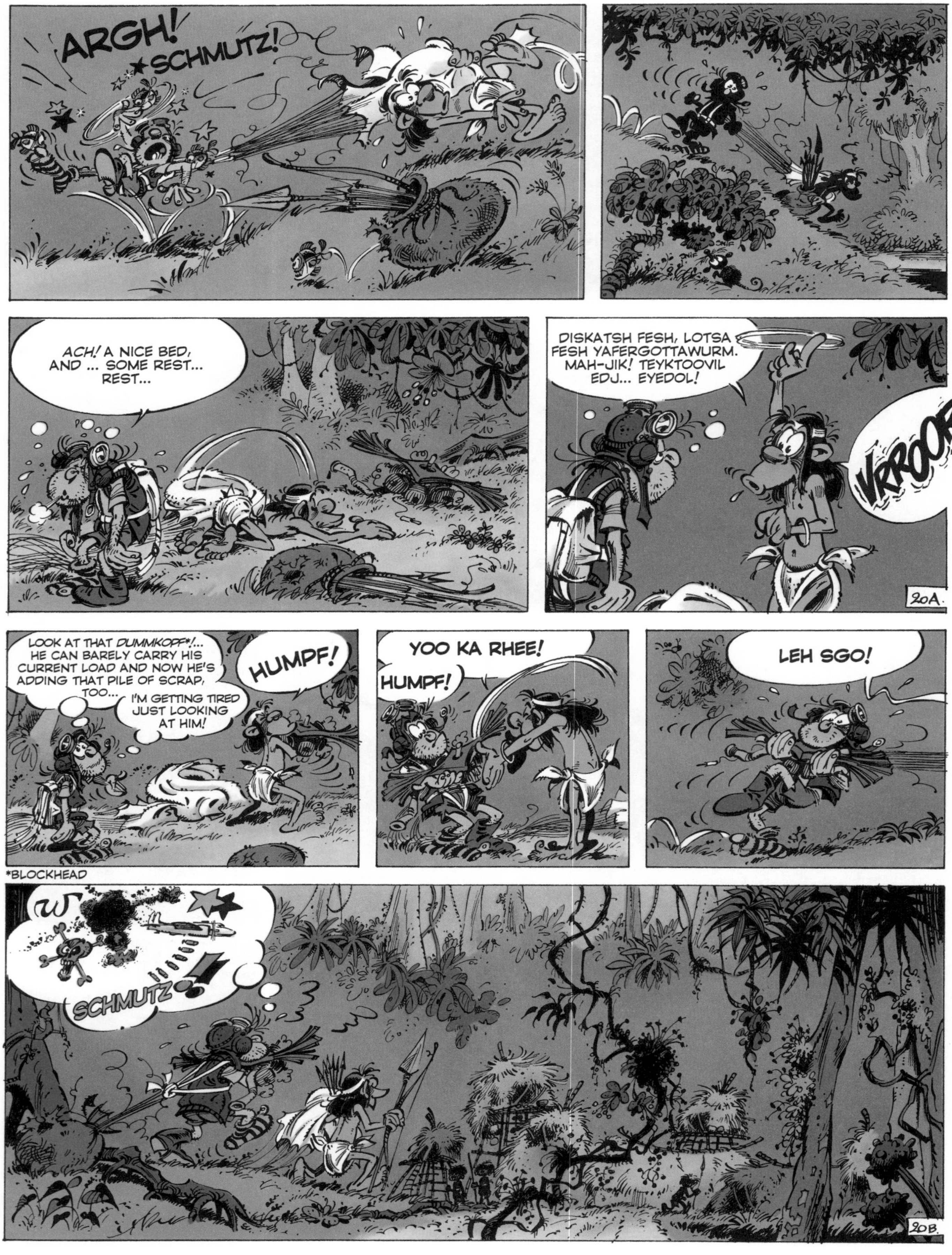
ARGH!
★SCHMUTZ!
ACH! A NICE BED, AND ... SOME REST... REST...
DISKATSH FESH, LOTSA FESH YAFERGOTTAWURM. MAH-JIK! TEYKTOOVIL EDJ... EYEDOL!
VRROOR
20A.
LOOK AT THAT DUMMKOPF*!... HE CAN BARELY CARRY HIS CURRENT LOAD AND NOW HE'S ADDING THAT PILE OF SCRAP, TOO...
I'M GETTING TIRED JUST LOOKING AT HIM!
HUMPF!
YOO KA RHEE!
HUMPF!
LEH SGO!
SCHMUTZ
20B.

*BLOCKHEAD

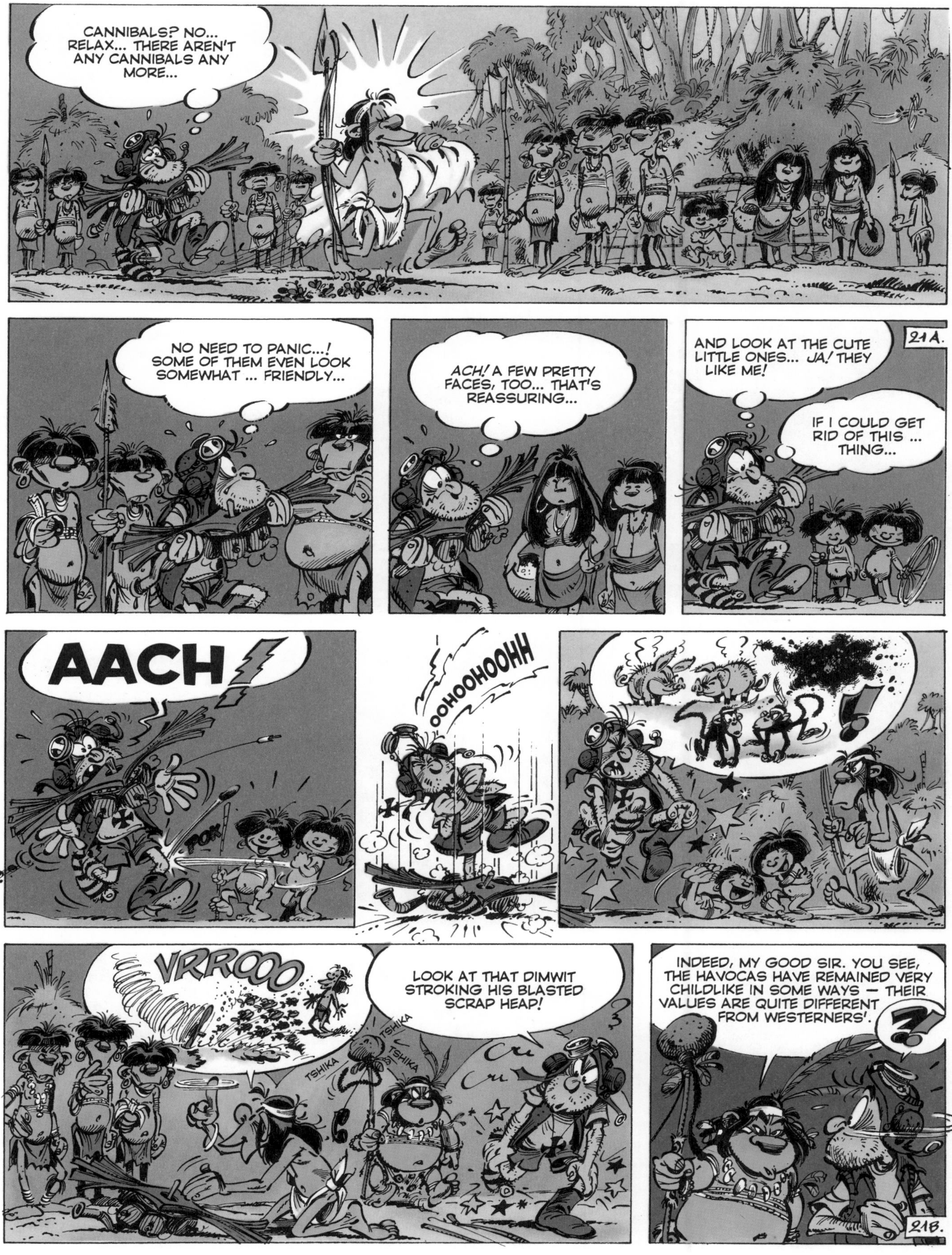
CANNIBALS? NO... RELAX... THERE AREN'T ANY CANNIBALS ANY MORE...
NO NEED TO PANIC...! SOME OF THEM EVEN LOOK SOMEWHAT ... FRIENDLY...
ACH! A FEW PRETTY FACES, TOO... THAT'S REASSURING...
21A.
AND LOOK AT THE CUTE LITTLE ONES... JA! THEY LIKE ME!
IF I COULD GET RID OF THIS ... THING...
AACH
POK
OOHOOHOOHH
VRROOO
TSHIKA TSHIKA
LOOK AT THAT DIMWIT STROKING HIS BLASTED SCRAP HEAP!
INDEED, MY GOOD SIR. YOU SEE, THE HAVOCAS HAVE REMAINED VERY CHILDLIKE IN SOME WAYS — THEIR VALUES ARE QUITE DIFFERENT FROM WESTERNERS'.
21B.

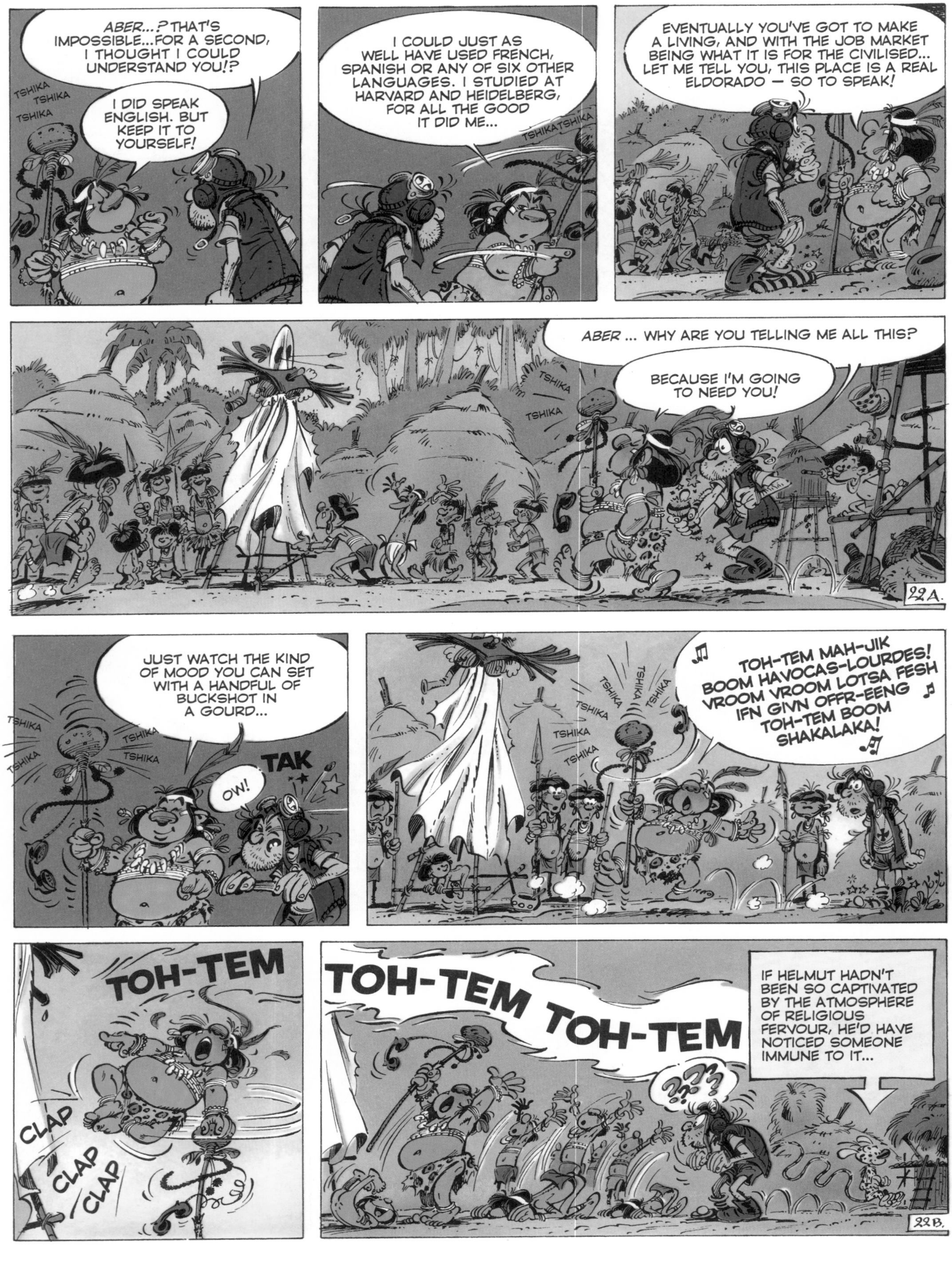
ABER...? THAT'S IMPOSSIBLE...FOR A SECOND, I THOUGHT I COULD UNDERSTAND YOU!?
TSHIKA TSHIKA TSHIKA
I DID SPEAK ENGLISH. BUT KEEP IT TO YOURSELF!
I COULD JUST AS WELL HAVE USED FRENCH, SPANISH OR ANY OF SIX OTHER LANGUAGES. I STUDIED AT HARVARD AND HEIDELBERG, FOR ALL THE GOOD IT DID ME...
TSHIKATSHIKA
EVENTUALLY YOU'VE GOT TO MAKE A LIVING, AND WITH THE JOB MARKET BEING WHAT IT IS FOR THE CIVILISED... LET ME TELL YOU, THIS PLACE IS A REAL ELDORADO — SO TO SPEAK!
ABER ... WHY ARE YOU TELLING ME ALL THIS?
TSHIKA
TSHIKA
BECAUSE I'M GOING TO NEED YOU!
22A.
JUST WATCH THE KIND OF MOOD YOU CAN SET WITH A HANDFUL OF BUCKSHOT IN A GOURD...
TSHIKA TSHIKA TSHIKA TSHIKA
TAK
OW!
TSHIKA TSHIKA TSHIKA TSHIKA TSHIKA
TOH-TEM MAH-JIK BOOM HAVOCAS-LOURDES! VROOM VROOM LOTSA FESH IFN GIVN OFFR-EENG TOH-TEM BOOM SHAKALAKA!
TOH-TEM
CLAP
CLAP
CLAP
TOH-TEM TOH-TEM TOH-TEM
IF HELMUT HADN'T BEEN SO CAPTIVATED BY THE ATMOSPHERE OF RELIGIOUS FERVOUR, HE'D HAVE NOTICED SOMEONE IMMUNE TO IT...
22B.

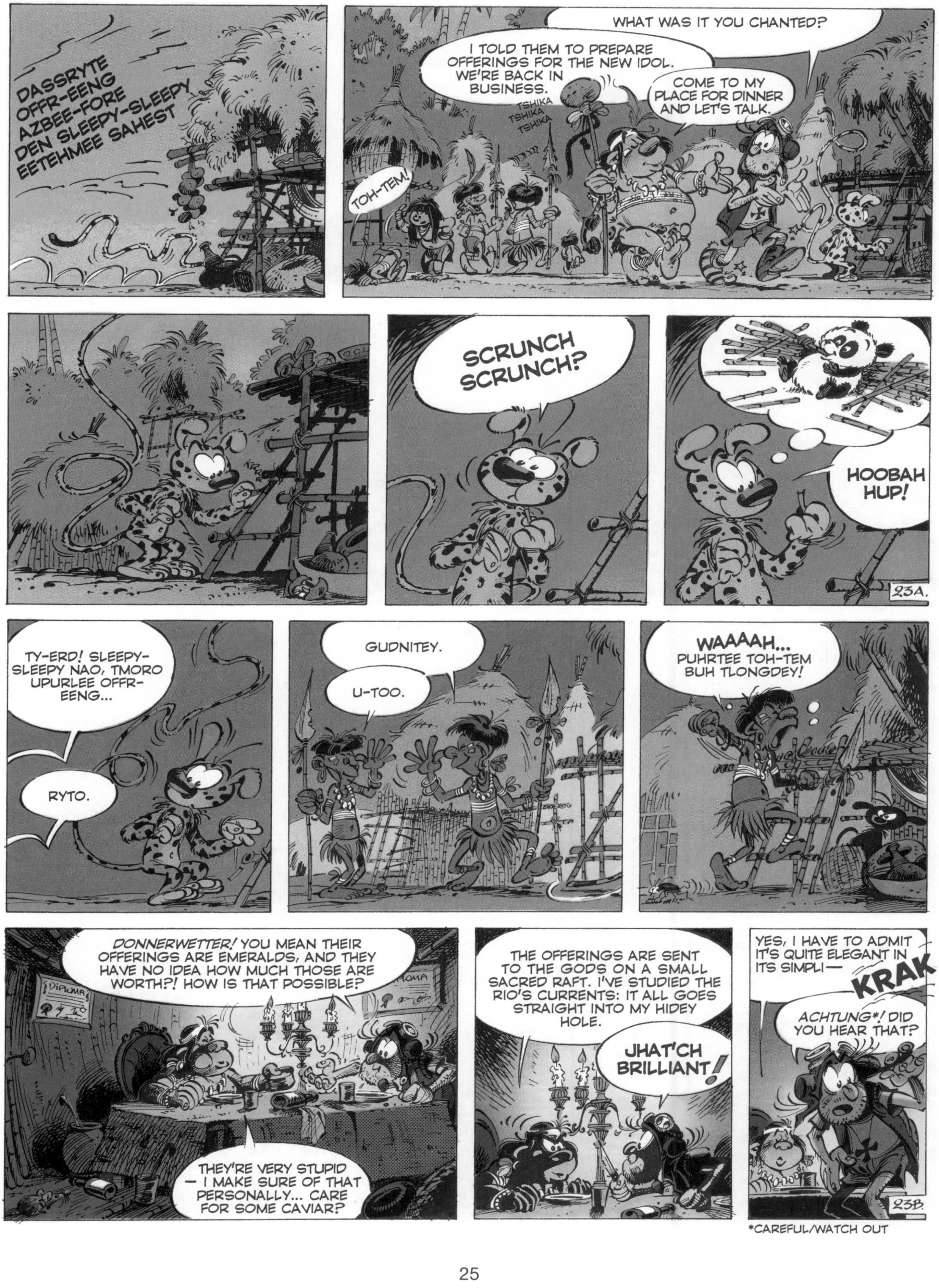
DASSRYTE OFFR-EENG AZBEE-FORE DEN SLEEPY-SLEEPY EETEHMEE SAHEST
WHAT WAS IT YOU CHANTED?
I TOLD THEM TO PREPARE OFFERINGS FOR THE NEW IDOL. WE'RE BACK IN BUSINESS.
COME TO MY PLACE FOR DINNER AND LET'S TALK.
TSHIKA TSHIKA TSHIKA
TOH-TEM!
SCRUNCH SCRUNCH?
HOOBAH HUP!
23A.
TY-ERD! SLEEPY-SLEEPY NAO, TMORO UPURLEE OFFR-EENG...
RYTO.
GUDNITEY.
U-TOO.
WAAAAH... PUHRTEE TOH-TEM BUH TLONGDEY!
DONNERWETTER! YOU MEAN THEIR OFFERINGS ARE EMERALDS, AND THEY HAVE NO IDEA HOW MUCH THOSE ARE WORTH?! HOW IS THAT POSSIBLE?
DIPLOMA
THEY'RE VERY STUPID — I MAKE SURE OF THAT PERSONALLY... CARE FOR SOME CAVIAR?
THE OFFERINGS ARE SENT TO THE GODS ON A SMALL SACRED RAFT. I'VE STUDIED THE RIO'S CURRENTS: IT ALL GOES STRAIGHT INTO MY HIDEY HOLE.
JHAT'CH BRILLIANT!
YES, I HAVE TO ADMIT IT'S QUITE ELEGANT IN ITS SIMPLI—
KRAK
ACHTUNG*! DID YOU HEAR THAT?
23B.

*CAREFUL/WATCH OUT

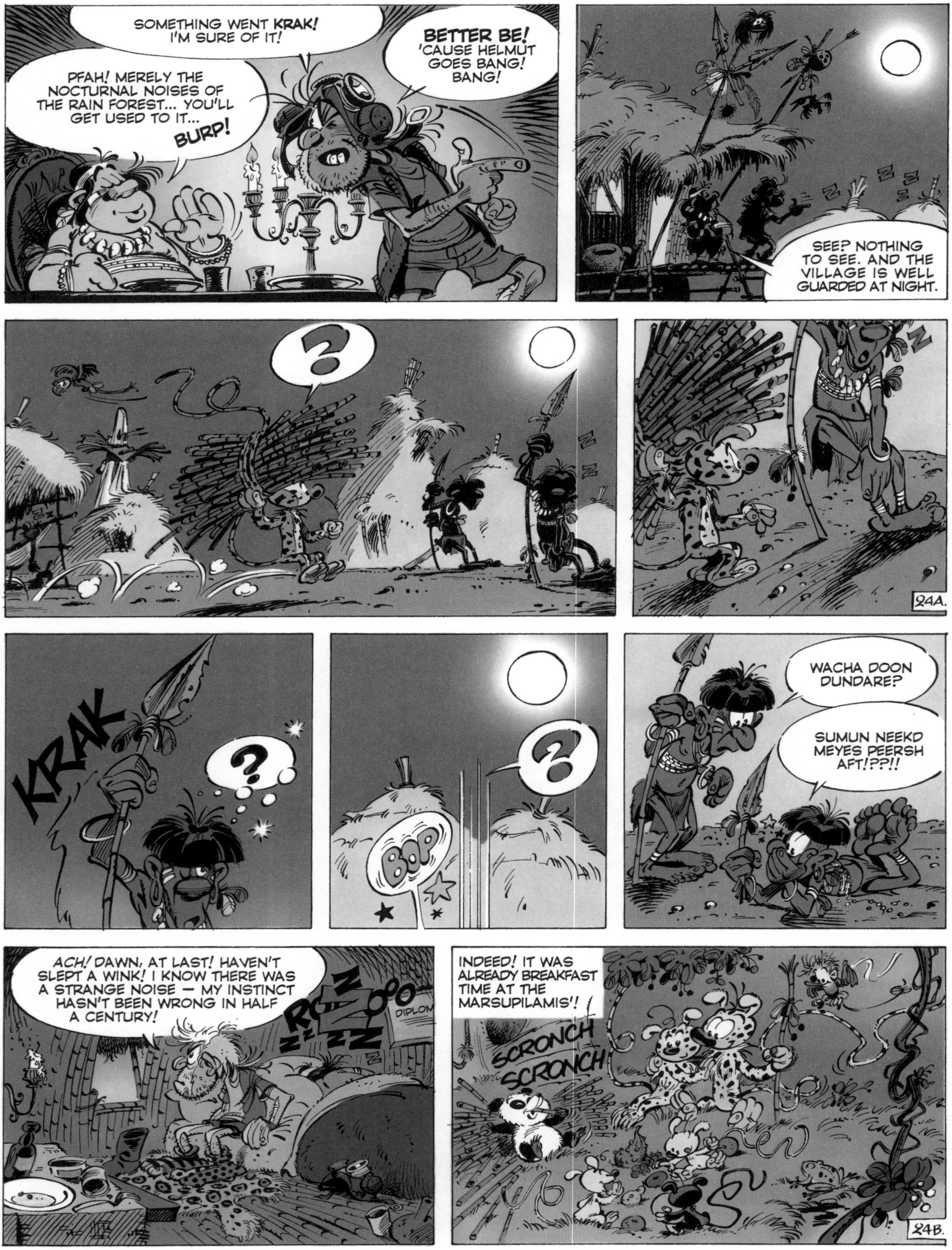
SOMETHING WENT KRAK! I'M SURE OF IT!
PFAH! MERELY THE NOCTURNAL NOISES OF THE RAIN FOREST... YOU'LL GET USED TO IT... BURP!
BETTER BE! 'CAUSE HELMUT GOES BANG! BANG!
SEE? NOTHING TO SEE. AND THE VILLAGE IS WELL GUARDED AT NIGHT.
24A.
KRAK
BOP
WACHA DOON DUNDARE?
SUMUN NEEKD MEYES PEERSH AFT!??!!
ACH! DAWN, AT LAST! HAVEN'T SLEPT A WINK! I KNOW THERE WAS A STRANGE NOISE — MY INSTINCT HASN'T BEEN WRONG IN HALF A CENTURY!
DIPLOM
INDEED! IT WAS ALREADY BREAKFAST TIME AT THE MARSUPILAMIS'!
SCRONCH
SCRONCH
24B.

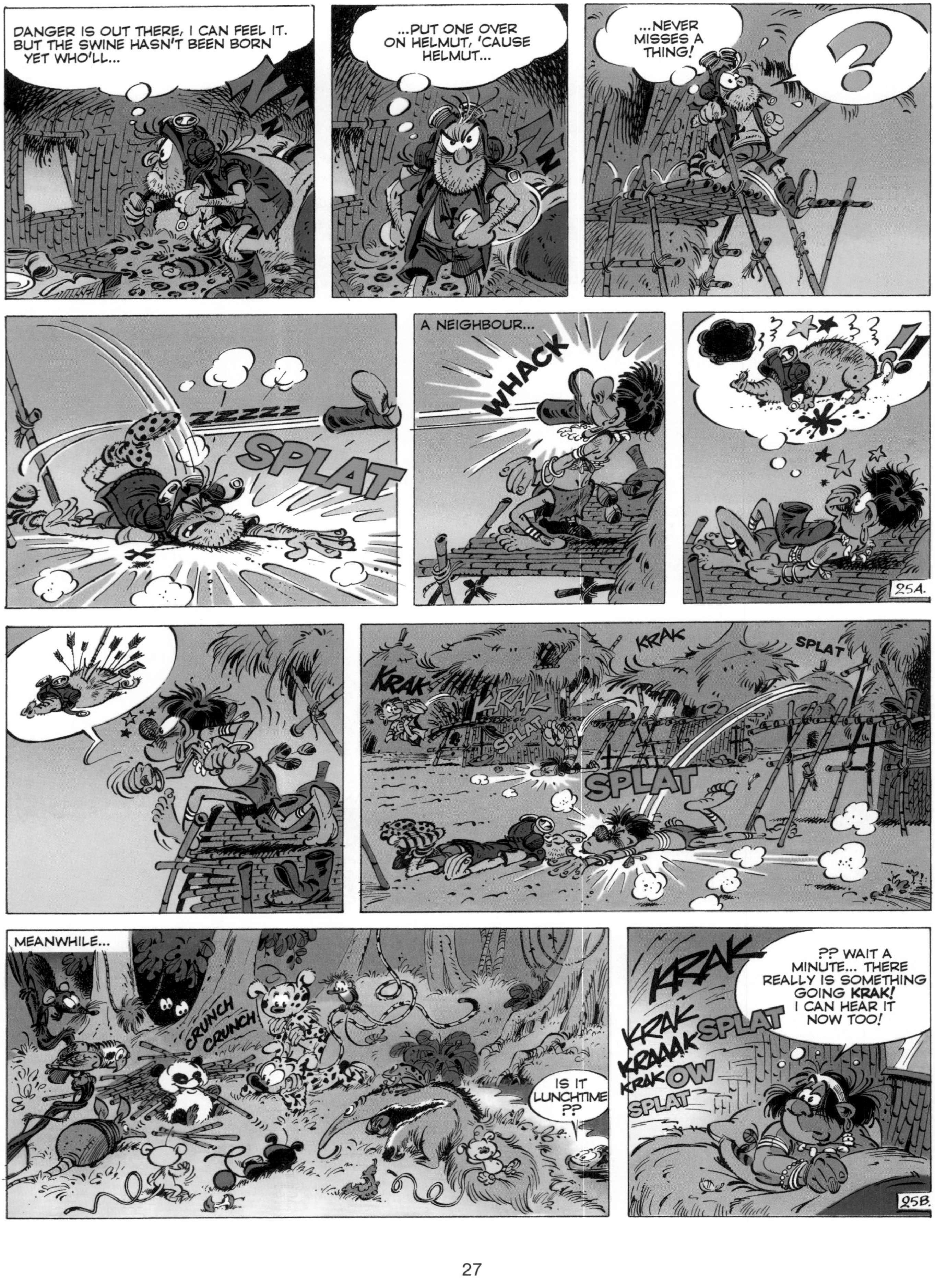
DANGER IS OUT THERE, I CAN FEEL IT. BUT THE SWINE HASN'T BEEN BORN YET WHO'LL...
...PUT ONE OVER ON HELMUT, 'CAUSE HELMUT...
...NEVER MISSES A THING!
?
ZZZZZ
SPLAT
A NEIGHBOUR...
WHACK
25A.
KRAK
KRAK
KRAK
SPLAT
SPLAT
SPLAT
MEANWHILE...
CRUNCH
CRUNCH
IS IT LUNCHTIME ??
KRAK
KRAK
KRAAAK
KRAK
SPLAT
OW
SPLAT
?? WAIT A MINUTE... THERE REALLY IS SOMETHING GOING **KRAK!** I CAN HEAR IT NOW TOO!
25B.

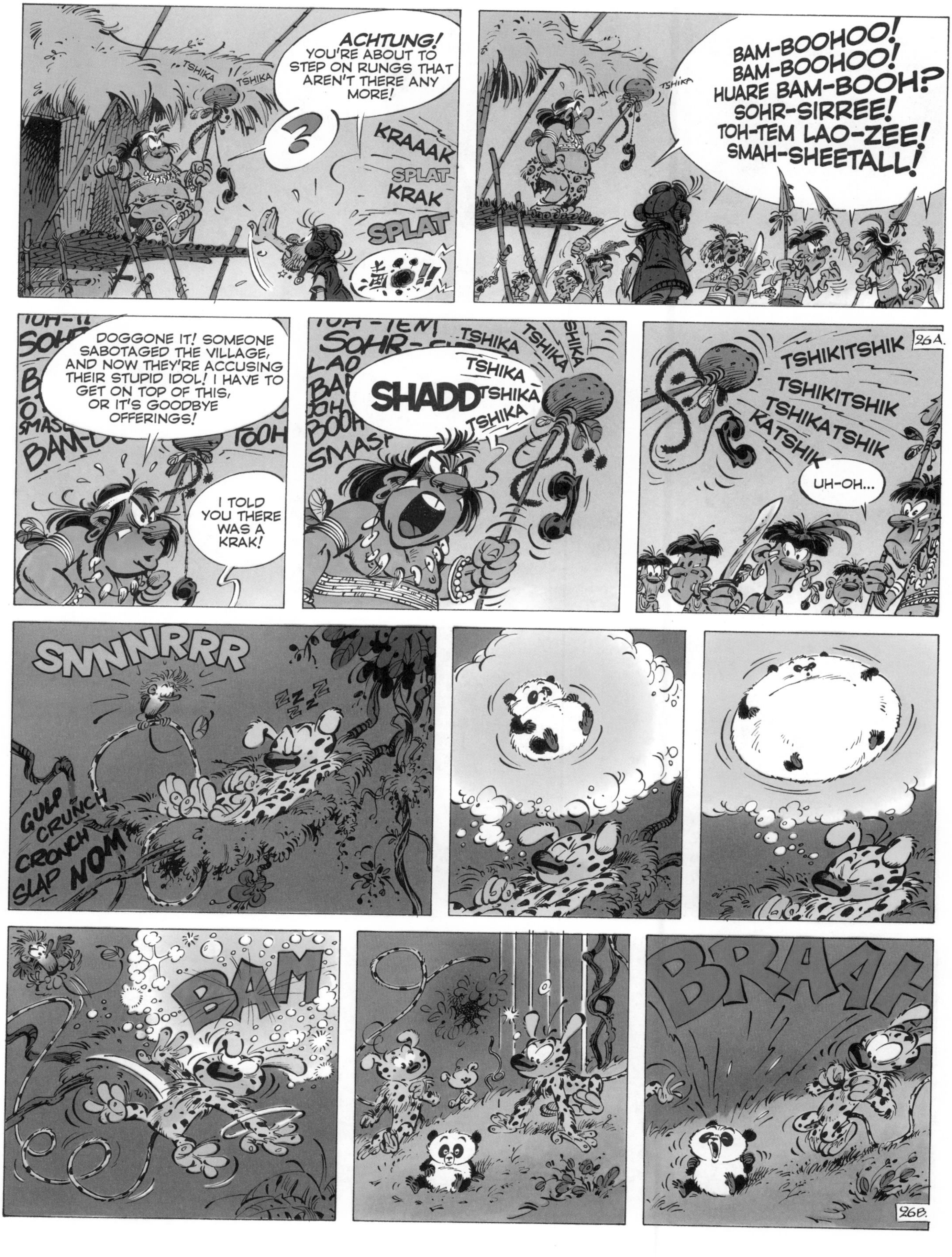
TSHIKA
TSHIKA
ACHTUNG! YOU'RE ABOUT TO STEP ON RUNGS THAT AREN'T THERE ANY MORE!
?
KRAAAK
SPLAT
KRAK
SPLAT
TSHIKA
BAM-BOOHOO! BAM-BOOHOO! HUARE BAM-BOOH? SOHR-SIRREE! TOH-TEM LAO-ZEE! SMAH-SHEETALL!
DOGGONE IT! SOMEONE SABOTAGED THE VILLAGE, AND NOW THEY'RE ACCUSING THEIR STUPID IDOL! I HAVE TO GET ON TOP OF THIS, OR IT'S GOODBYE OFFERINGS!
I TOLD YOU THERE WAS A KRAK!
TSHIKA
TSHIKA
TSHIKA
TSHIKA
SHADD
TSHIKA
TSHIKA
26A.
TSHIKITSHIK
TSHIKITSHIK
TSHIKATSHIK
KATSHIK
UH-OH...
SNNNRRR
GULP
CRUNCH
CRONCH
SLAP
NOM
BAM
BRAAH
26B.

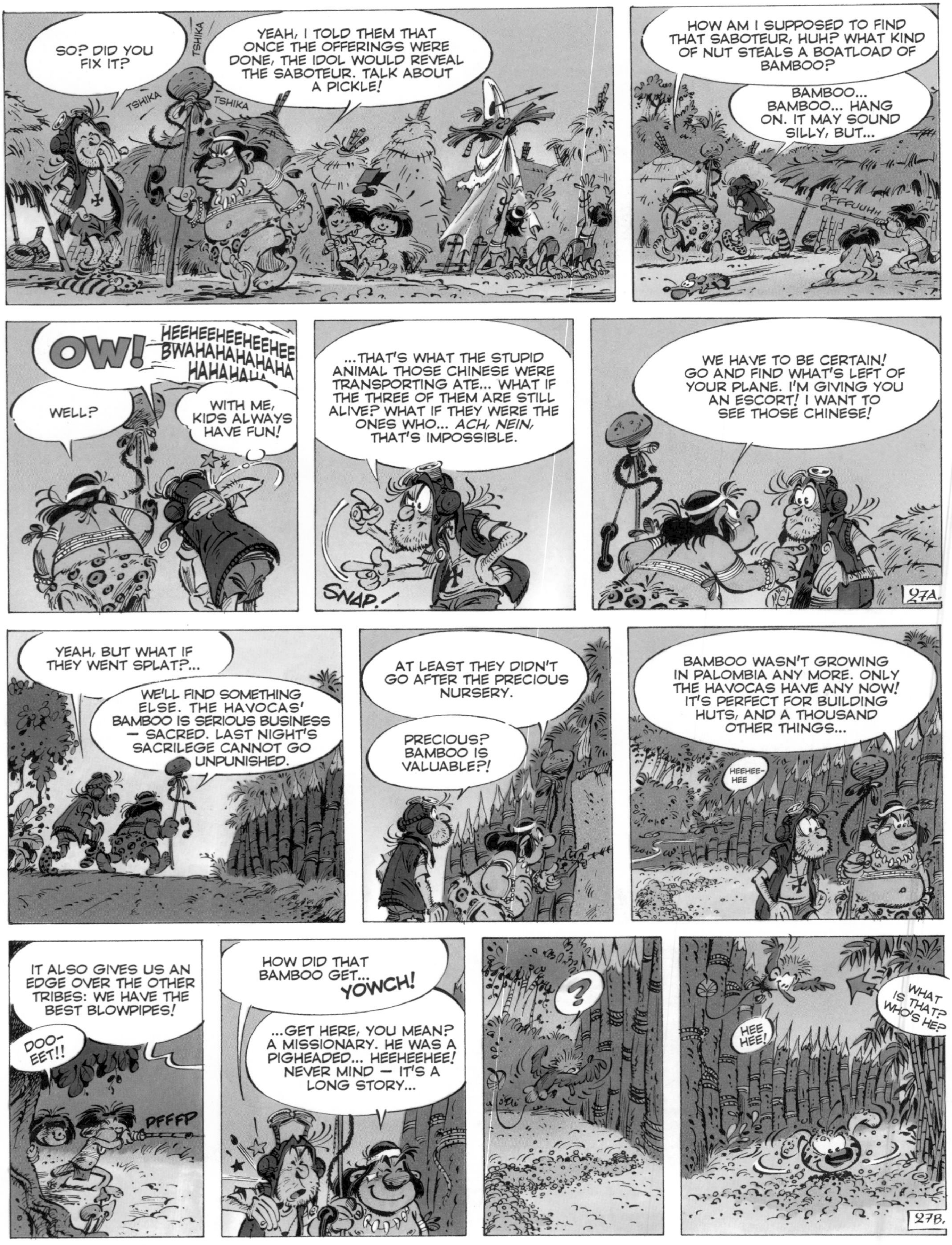
SO? DID YOU FIX IT?
TSHIKA
TSHIKA
TSHIKA
YEAH, I TOLD THEM THAT ONCE THE OFFERINGS WERE DONE, THE IDOL WOULD REVEAL THE SABOTEUR. TALK ABOUT A PICKLE!
HOW AM I SUPPOSED TO FIND THAT SABOTEUR, HUH? WHAT KIND OF NUT STEALS A BOATLOAD OF BAMBOO?
BAMBOO... BAMBOO... HANG ON. IT MAY SOUND SILLY, BUT...
PFFFUUHH
OW!
HEEHEEHEEHEEHEE BWAHAHAHAHAHEE HAHAHAHA
WELL?
WITH ME, KIDS ALWAYS HAVE FUN!
...THAT'S WHAT THE STUPID ANIMAL THOSE CHINESE WERE TRANSPORTING ATE... WHAT IF THE THREE OF THEM ARE STILL ALIVE? WHAT IF THEY WERE THE ONES WHO... *ACH, NEIN,* THAT'S IMPOSSIBLE.
SNAP!
WE HAVE TO BE CERTAIN! GO AND FIND WHAT'S LEFT OF YOUR PLANE. I'M GIVING YOU AN ESCORT! I WANT TO SEE THOSE CHINESE!
27A.
YEAH, BUT WHAT IF THEY WENT SPLAT?...
WE'LL FIND SOMETHING ELSE. THE HAVOCAS' BAMBOO IS SERIOUS BUSINESS — SACRED. LAST NIGHT'S SACRILEGE CANNOT GO UNPUNISHED.
AT LEAST THEY DIDN'T GO AFTER THE PRECIOUS NURSERY.
PRECIOUS? BAMBOO IS VALUABLE?!
BAMBOO WASN'T GROWING IN PALOMBIA ANY MORE. ONLY THE HAVOCAS HAVE ANY NOW! IT'S PERFECT FOR BUILDING HUTS, AND A THOUSAND OTHER THINGS...
HEEHEE-HEE
IT ALSO GIVES US AN EDGE OVER THE OTHER TRIBES: WE HAVE THE BEST BLOWPIPES!
DOO-EET!!
PFFFP
HOW DID THAT BAMBOO GET... YOWCH!
...GET HERE, YOU MEAN? A MISSIONARY. HE WAS A PIGHEADED... HEEHEEHEE! NEVER MIND — IT'S A LONG STORY...
?
HEE HEE!
WHAT IS THAT? WHO'S HE?
27B.

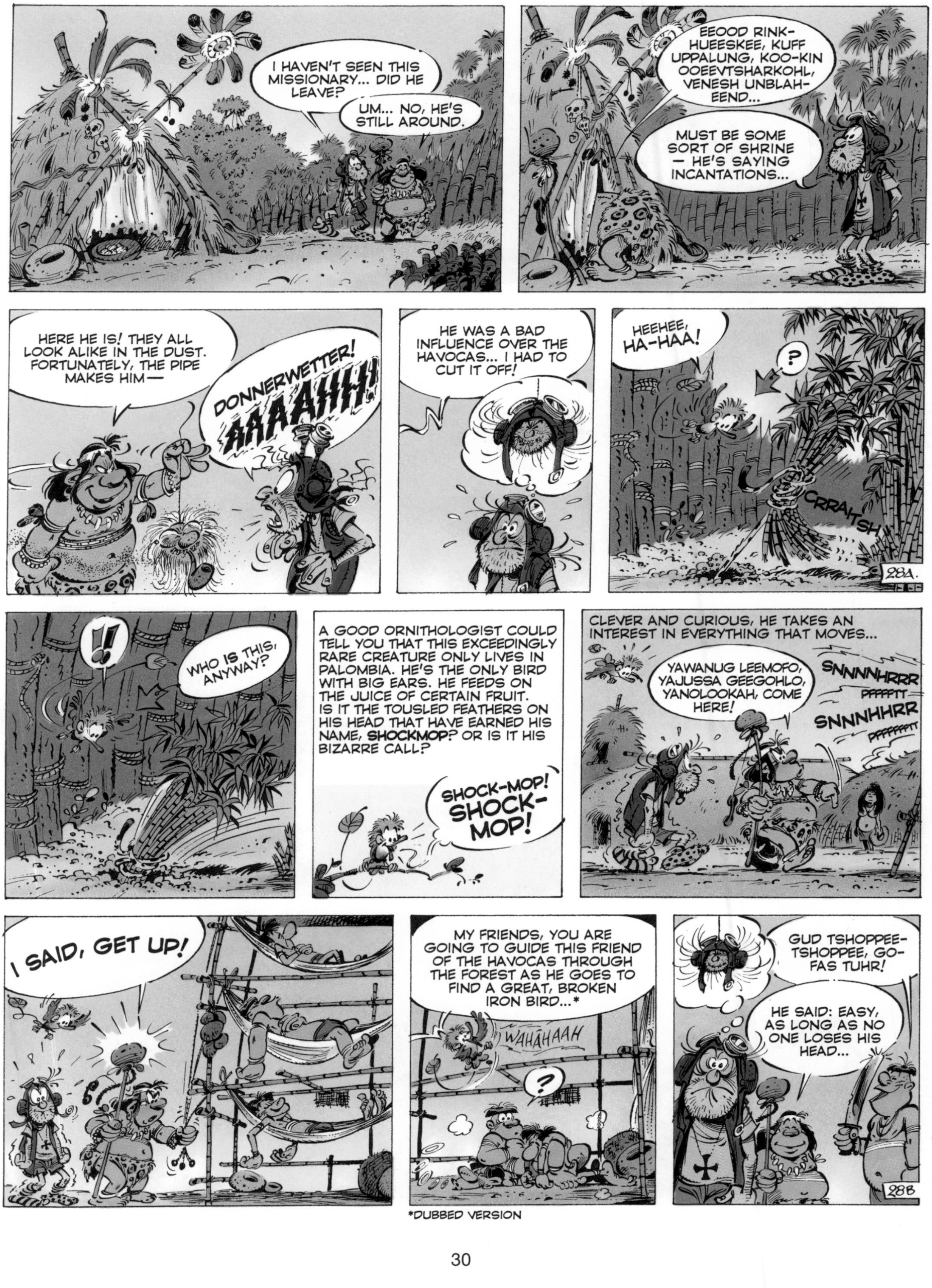
I HAVEN'T SEEN THIS MISSIONARY... DID HE LEAVE?
UM... NO, HE'S STILL AROUND.
EEOOD RINK-HUEESKEE, KUFF UPPALUNG, KOO-KIN OOEEVTSHARKOHL, VENESH UNBLAH-EEND...
MUST BE SOME SORT OF SHRINE — HE'S SAYING INCANTATIONS...
HERE HE IS! THEY ALL LOOK ALIKE IN THE DUST. FORTUNATELY, THE PIPE MAKES HIM—
DONNERWETTER!
AAAAHHH!
HE WAS A BAD INFLUENCE OVER THE HAVOCAS... I HAD TO CUT IT OFF!
HEEHEE, HA-HAA!
?
CRRAITSH
28A.
!!
WHO IS THIS, ANYWAY?
A GOOD ORNITHOLOGIST COULD TELL YOU THAT THIS EXCEEDINGLY RARE CREATURE ONLY LIVES IN PALOMBIA. HE'S THE ONLY BIRD WITH BIG EARS. HE FEEDS ON THE JUICE OF CERTAIN FRUIT. IS IT THE TOUSLED FEATHERS ON HIS HEAD THAT HAVE EARNED HIS NAME, SHOCKMOP? OR IS IT HIS BIZARRE CALL?
SHOCK-MOP! SHOCK-MOP!
CLEVER AND CURIOUS, HE TAKES AN INTEREST IN EVERYTHING THAT MOVES...
YAWANUG LEEMOFO, YAJUSSA GEEGOHLO, YANOLOOKAH, COME HERE!
SNNNNHRRR
PFFFFTT
SNNNHHRR
PFFFFFFTT
I SAID, GET UP!
MY FRIENDS, YOU ARE GOING TO GUIDE THIS FRIEND OF THE HAVOCAS THROUGH THE FOREST AS HE GOES TO FIND A GREAT, BROKEN IRON BIRD...*
WAHAHAAH
?
GUD TSHOPPEE-TSHOPPEE, GO-FAS TUHR!
HE SAID: EASY, AS LONG AS NO ONE LOSES HIS HEAD...
28B

*DUBBED VERSION

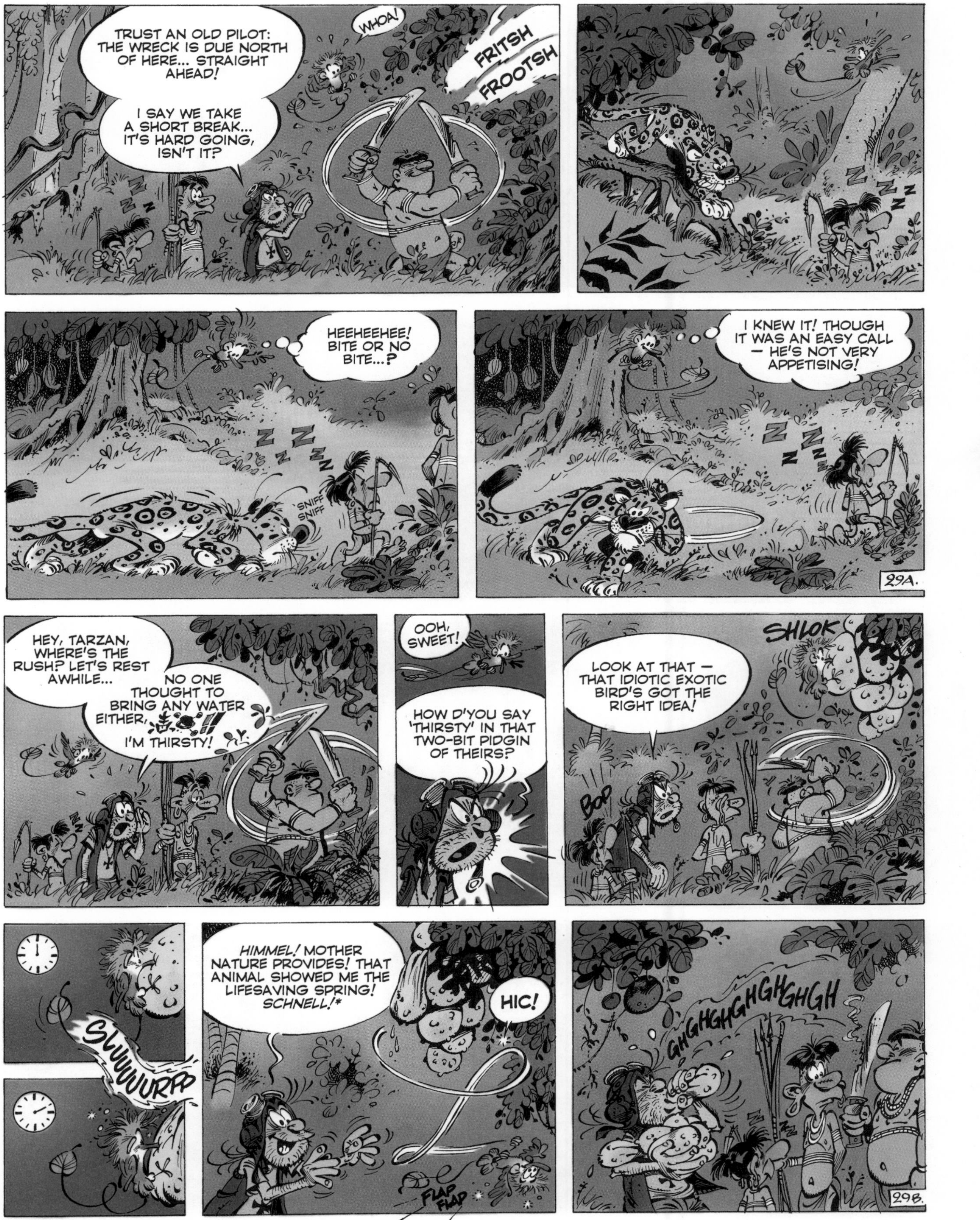
TRUST AN OLD PILOT: THE WRECK IS DUE NORTH OF HERE... STRAIGHT AHEAD!
I SAY WE TAKE A SHORT BREAK... IT'S HARD GOING, ISN'T IT?
WHOA!
FRITSH
FROOTSH
HEEHEEHEE! BITE OR NO BITE...?
SNIFF SNIFF
I KNEW IT! THOUGH IT WAS AN EASY CALL — HE'S NOT VERY APPETISING!
29A.
HEY, TARZAN, WHERE'S THE RUSH? LET'S REST AWHILE...
NO ONE THOUGHT TO BRING ANY WATER EITHER,
I'M THIRSTY!
OOH, SWEET!
HOW D'YOU SAY 'THIRSTY' IN THAT TWO-BIT PIDGIN OF THEIRS?
SHLOK
LOOK AT THAT — THAT IDIOTIC EXOTIC BIRD'S GOT THE RIGHT IDEA!
BOP
SLUUUUURRP
HIMMEL! MOTHER NATURE PROVIDES! THAT ANIMAL SHOWED ME THE LIFESAVING SPRING! *SCHNELL!**
HIC!
FLAP FLAP
GHGHGHGHGHGHGHGH
29B.

*QUICK!

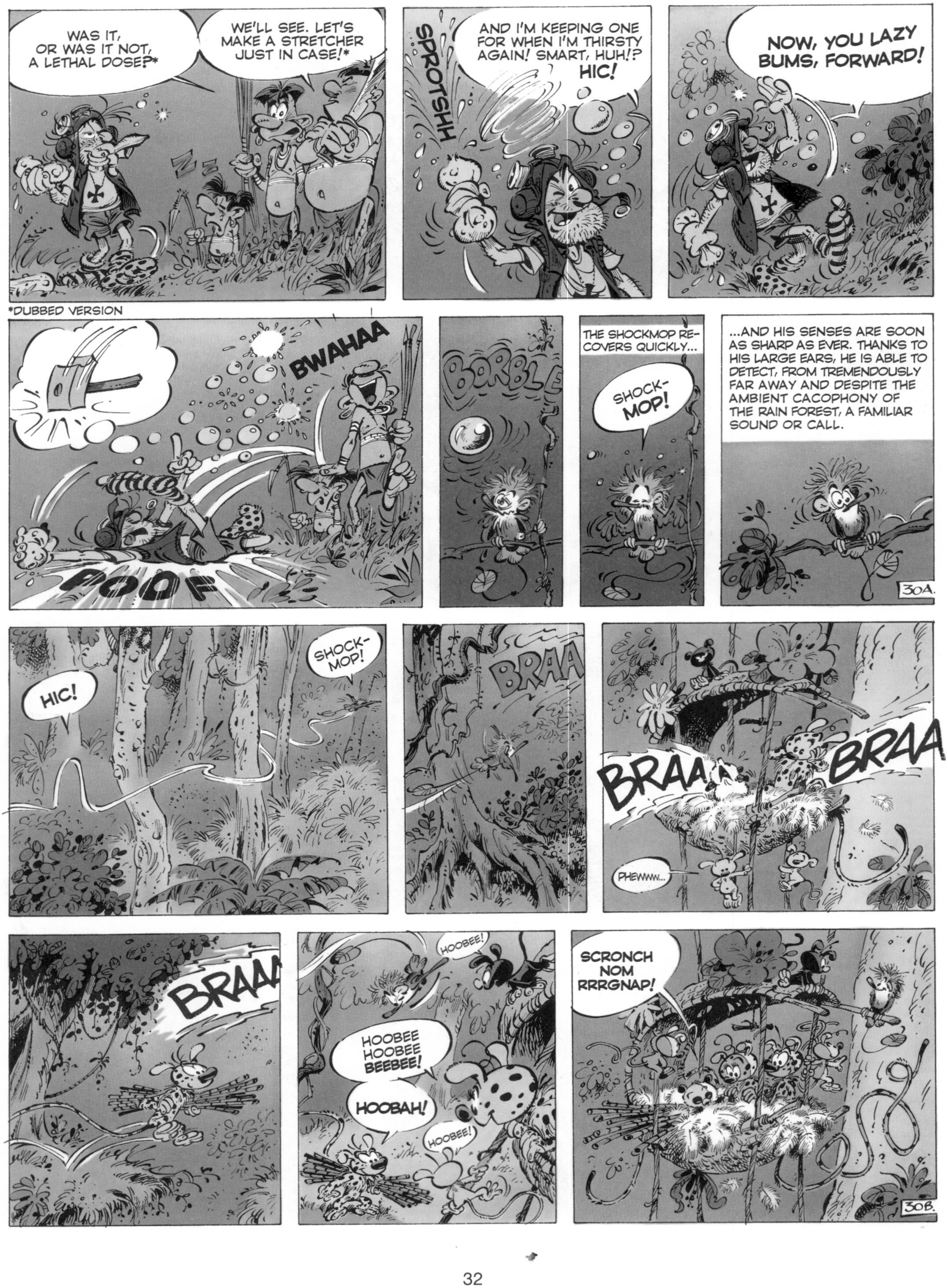
WAS IT, OR WAS IT NOT, A LETHAL DOSE?*
WE'LL SEE. LET'S MAKE A STRETCHER JUST IN CASE!*
SPROTSHH
AND I'M KEEPING ONE FOR WHEN I'M THIRSTY AGAIN! SMART, HUH!?
HIC!
NOW, YOU LAZY BUMS, FORWARD!
*DUBBED VERSION
BWAHAA
POOF
BORBLE
THE SHOCKMOP RECOVERS QUICKLY...
SHOCK-MOP!
...AND HIS SENSES ARE SOON AS SHARP AS EVER. THANKS TO HIS LARGE EARS, HE IS ABLE TO DETECT, FROM TREMENDOUSLY FAR AWAY AND DESPITE THE AMBIENT CACOPHONY OF THE RAIN FOREST, A FAMILIAR SOUND OR CALL.
30A.
HIC!
SHOCK-MOP!
BRAA
BRAA
BRAA
PHEWWW...
BRAA
HOOBEE!
HOOBEE HOOBEE BEEBEE!
HOOBAH!
HOOBEE!
SCRONCH NOM RRRGNAP!
30B.

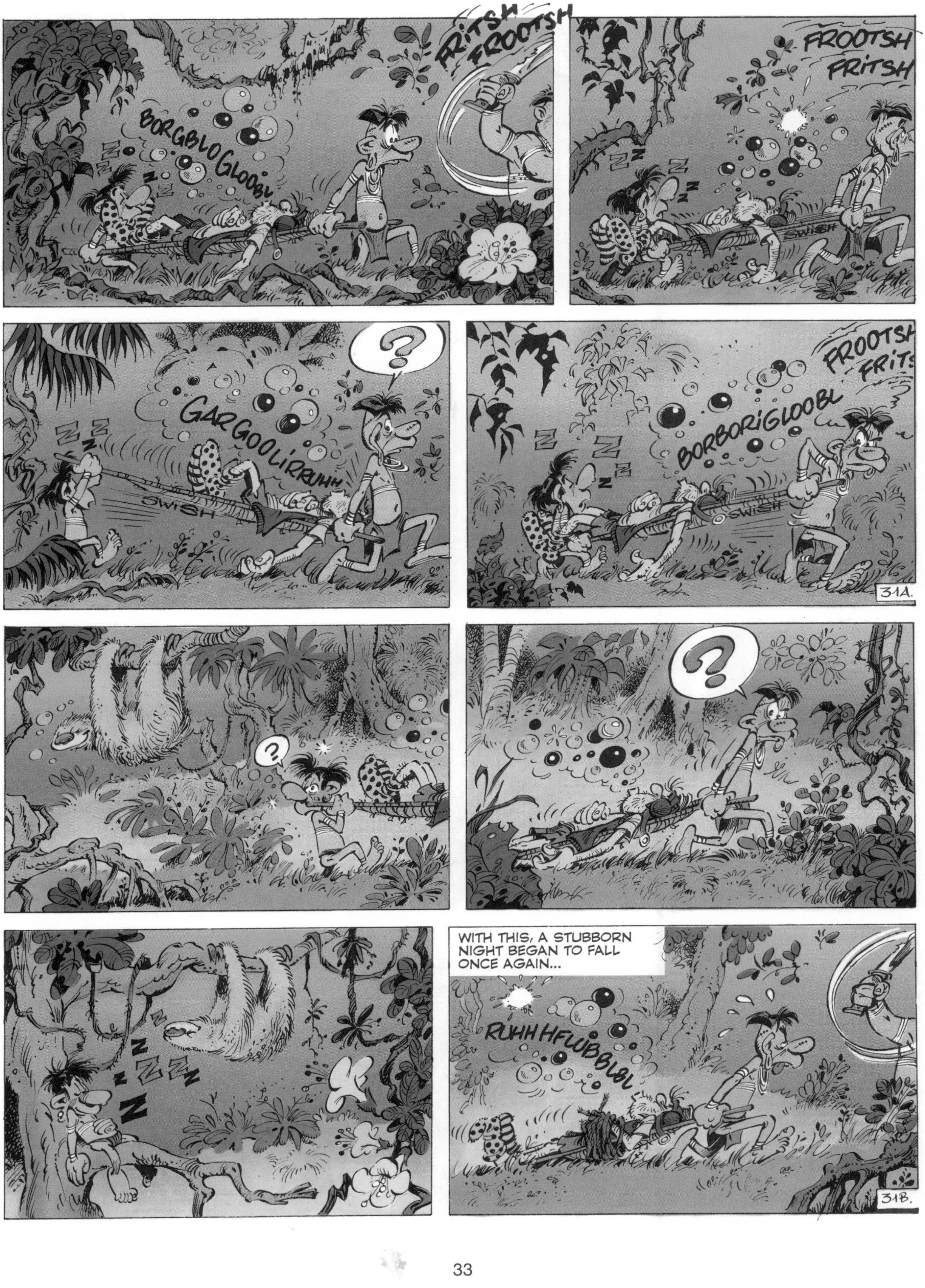
FRITSH
FROOTSH
BORGBLOGLOOBL
FROOTSH
FRITSH
SWISH
?
GARGOOLIRRUHH
SWISH
FROOTSH
FRITS
BORBORIGLOOBL
SWISH
31A.
?
?
WITH THIS, A STUBBORN NIGHT BEGAN TO FALL ONCE AGAIN...
RUHHHFLUBBLBL
31B.

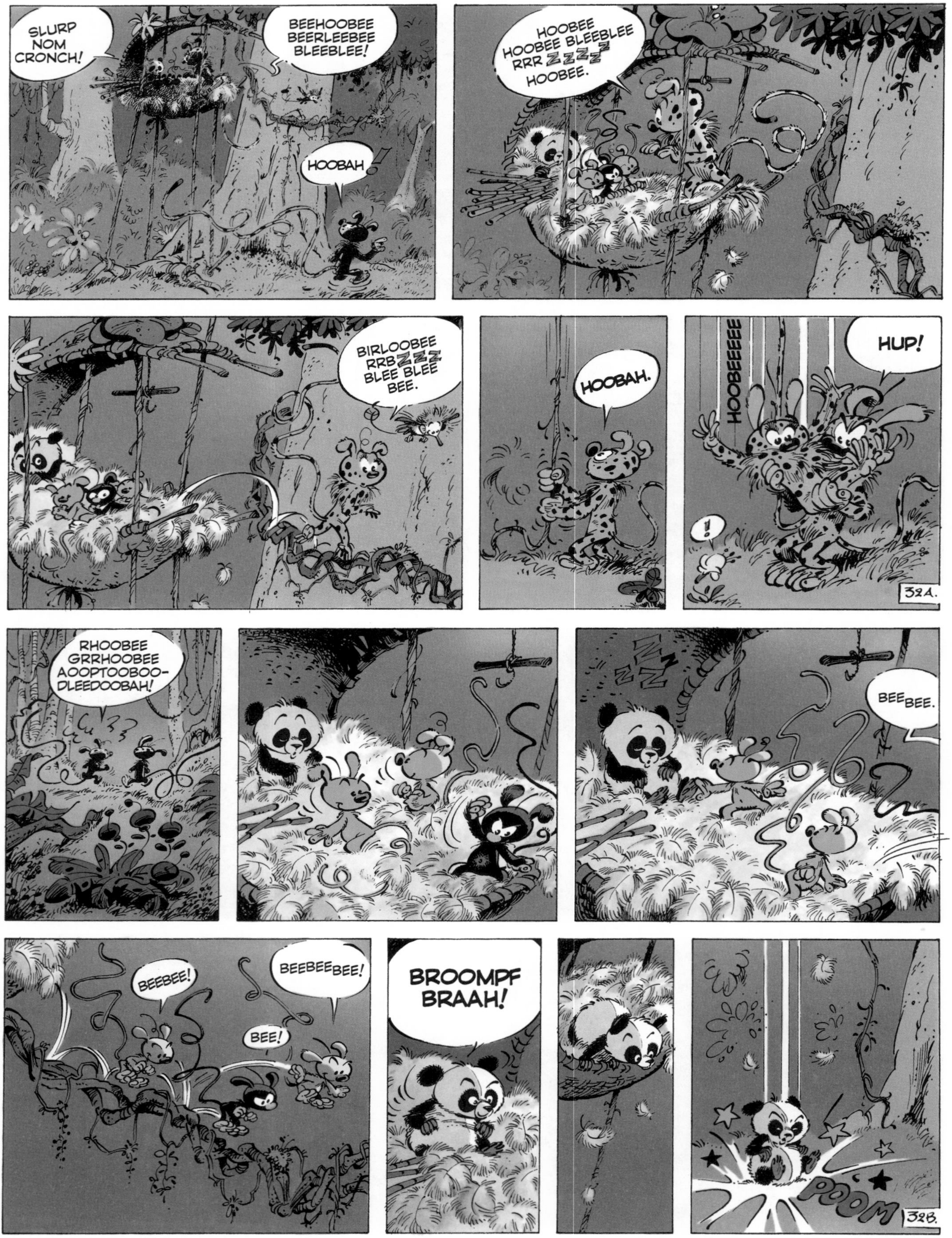
SLURP NOM CRONCH!
BEEHOOBEE BEERLEEBEE BLEEBLEE!
HOOBAH!
HOOBEE HOOBEE BLEEBLEE RRR ZZZZ HOOBEE.
BIRLOOBEE RRB ZZZ BLEE BLEE BEE.
HOOBAH.
HOOBEEEEE
HUP!
!
32A.
RHOOBEE GRRHOOBEE AOOPTOOBOO-DLEEDOOBAH!
ZZZ
BEEBEE.
BEEBEE!
BEEBEEBEE!
BEE!
BROOMPF BRAAH!
POOM
32B.

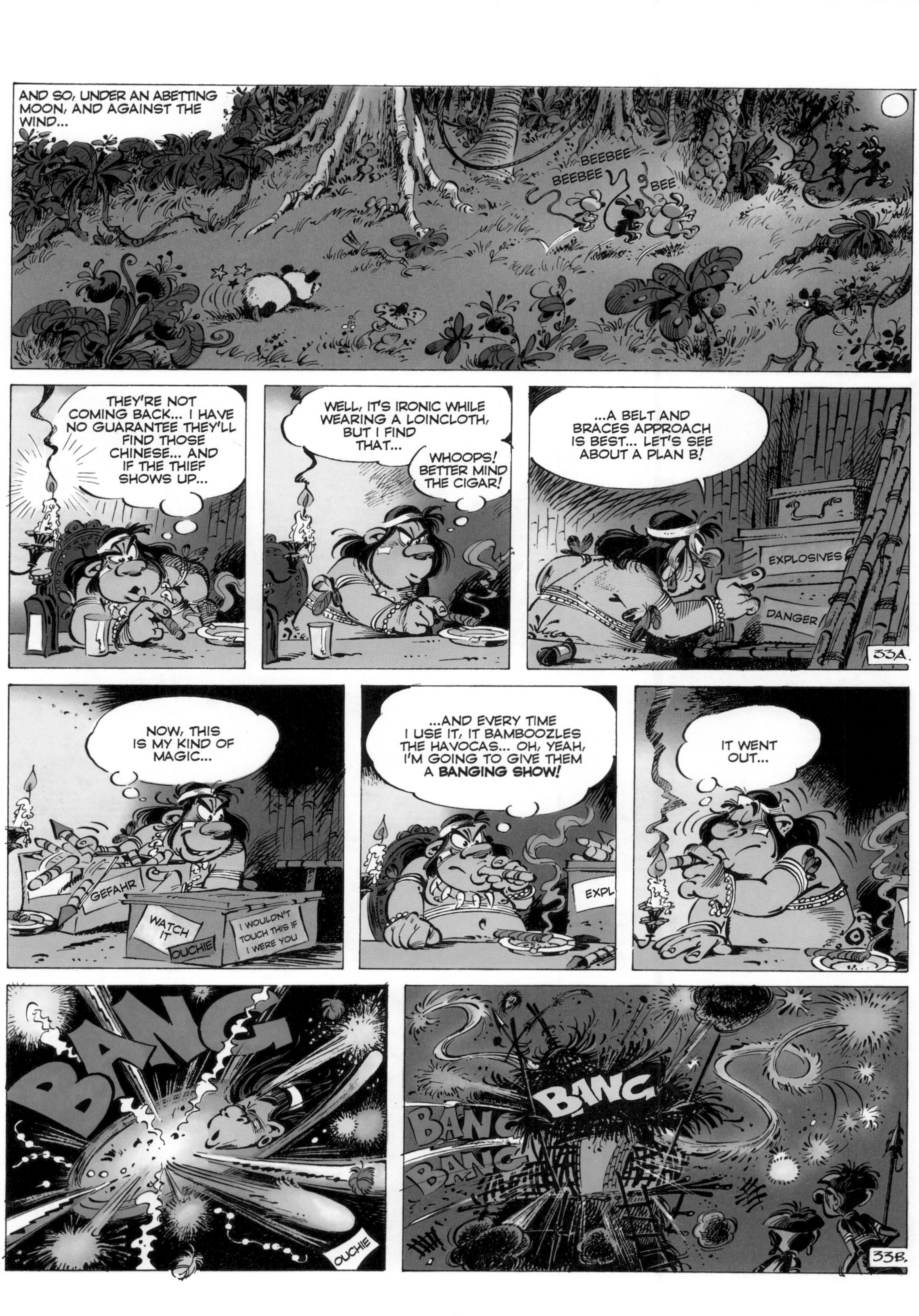
AND SO, UNDER AN ABETTING MOON, AND AGAINST THE WIND...
BEEBEE
BEEBEE
BEE
THEY'RE NOT COMING BACK... I HAVE NO GUARANTEE THEY'LL FIND THOSE CHINESE... AND IF THE THIEF SHOWS UP...
WELL, IT'S IRONIC WHILE WEARING A LOINCLOTH, BUT I FIND THAT...
WHOOPS! BETTER MIND THE CIGAR!
...A BELT AND BRACES APPROACH IS BEST... LET'S SEE ABOUT A PLAN B!
EXPLOSIVES
DANGER
33A.
NOW, THIS IS MY KIND OF MAGIC...
GEFAHR
WATCH IT
OUCHIE
I WOULDN'T TOUCH THIS IF I WERE YOU
...AND EVERY TIME I USE IT, IT BAMBOOZLES THE HAVOCAS... OH, YEAH, I'M GOING TO GIVE THEM A **BANGING SHOW!**
EXPL
IT WENT OUT...
BANG
OUCHIE
BANG
BANG
BANG
33B.

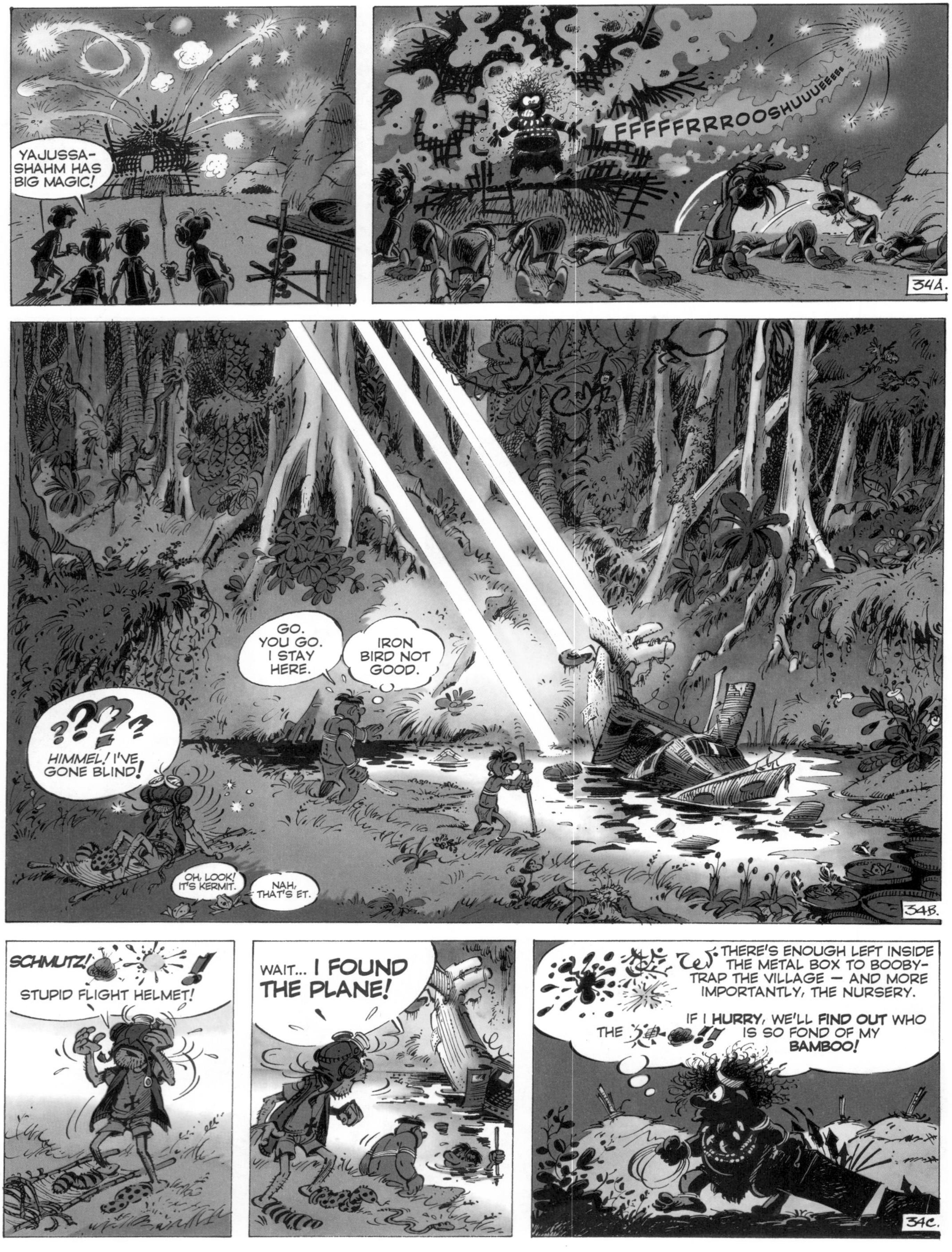
YAJUSSA-SHAHM HAS BIG MAGIC!
FFFFFRRROOSHUUUEEEE
34A.
GO. YOU GO. I STAY HERE.
IRON BIRD NOT GOOD.
???? HIMMEL! I'VE GONE BLIND!
OH, LOOK! IT'S KERMIT.
NAH, THAT'S ET.
34B.
SCHMUTZ!
STUPID FLIGHT HELMET!
WAIT... I FOUND THE PLANE!
THERE'S ENOUGH LEFT INSIDE THE METAL BOX TO BOOBY-TRAP THE VILLAGE — AND MORE IMPORTANTLY, THE NURSERY.
THE !!
IF I HURRY, WE'LL FIND OUT WHO IS SO FOND OF MY BAMBOO!
34C.

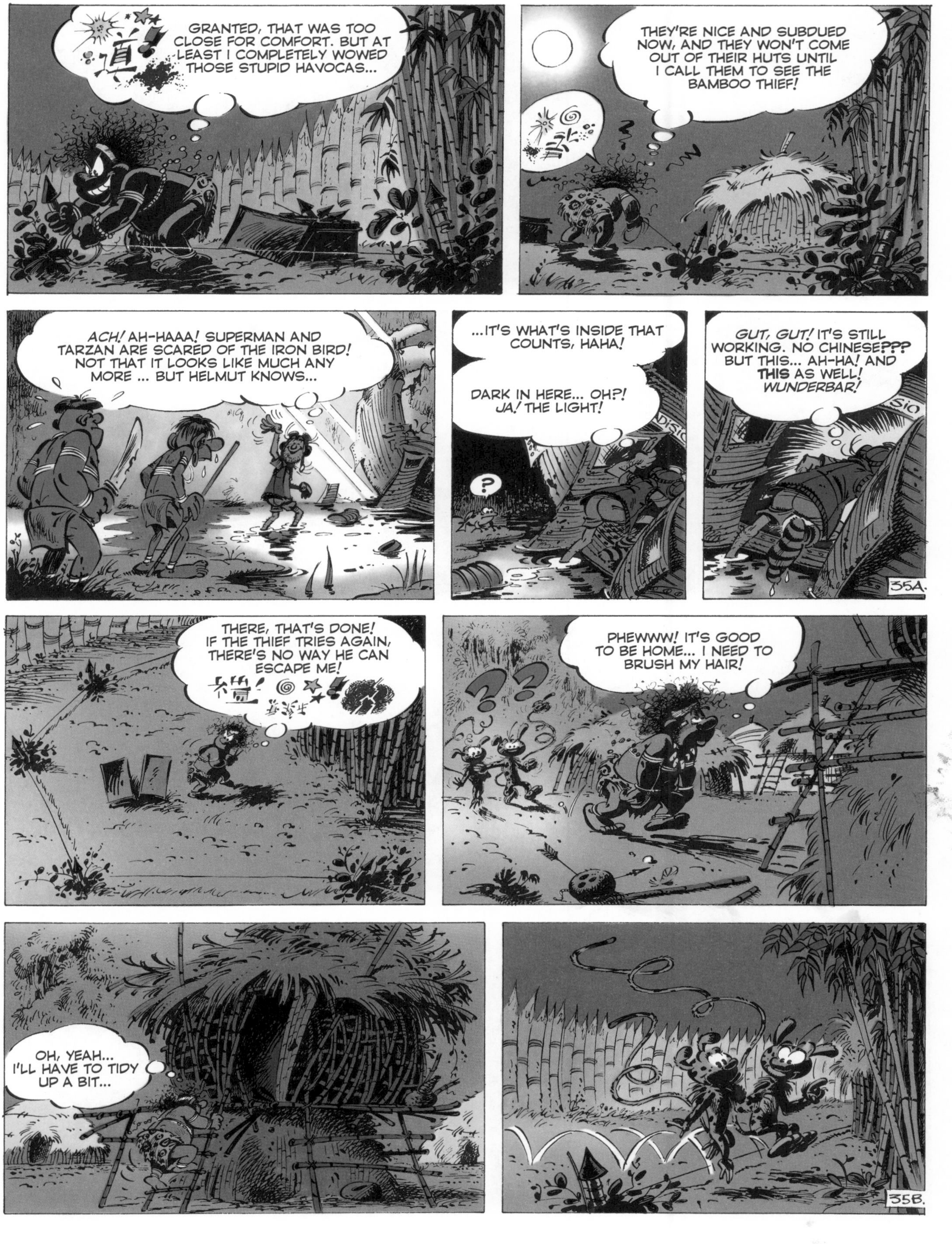
GRANTED, THAT WAS TOO CLOSE FOR COMFORT. BUT AT LEAST I COMPLETELY WOWED THOSE STUPID HAVOCAS...
THEY'RE NICE AND SUBDUED NOW, AND THEY WON'T COME OUT OF THEIR HUTS UNTIL I CALL THEM TO SEE THE BAMBOO THIEF!
ACH! AH-HAAA! SUPERMAN AND TARZAN ARE SCARED OF THE IRON BIRD! NOT THAT IT LOOKS LIKE MUCH ANY MORE ... BUT HELMUT KNOWS...
...IT'S WHAT'S INSIDE THAT COUNTS, HAHA!
DARK IN HERE... OH?! JA! THE LIGHT!
GUT, GUT! IT'S STILL WORKING. NO CHINESE??? BUT THIS... AH-HA! AND THIS AS WELL! WUNDERBAR!
35A.
THERE, THAT'S DONE! IF THE THIEF TRIES AGAIN, THERE'S NO WAY HE CAN ESCAPE ME!
PHEWWW! IT'S GOOD TO BE HOME... I NEED TO BRUSH MY HAIR!
OH, YEAH... I'LL HAVE TO TIDY UP A BIT...
35B.

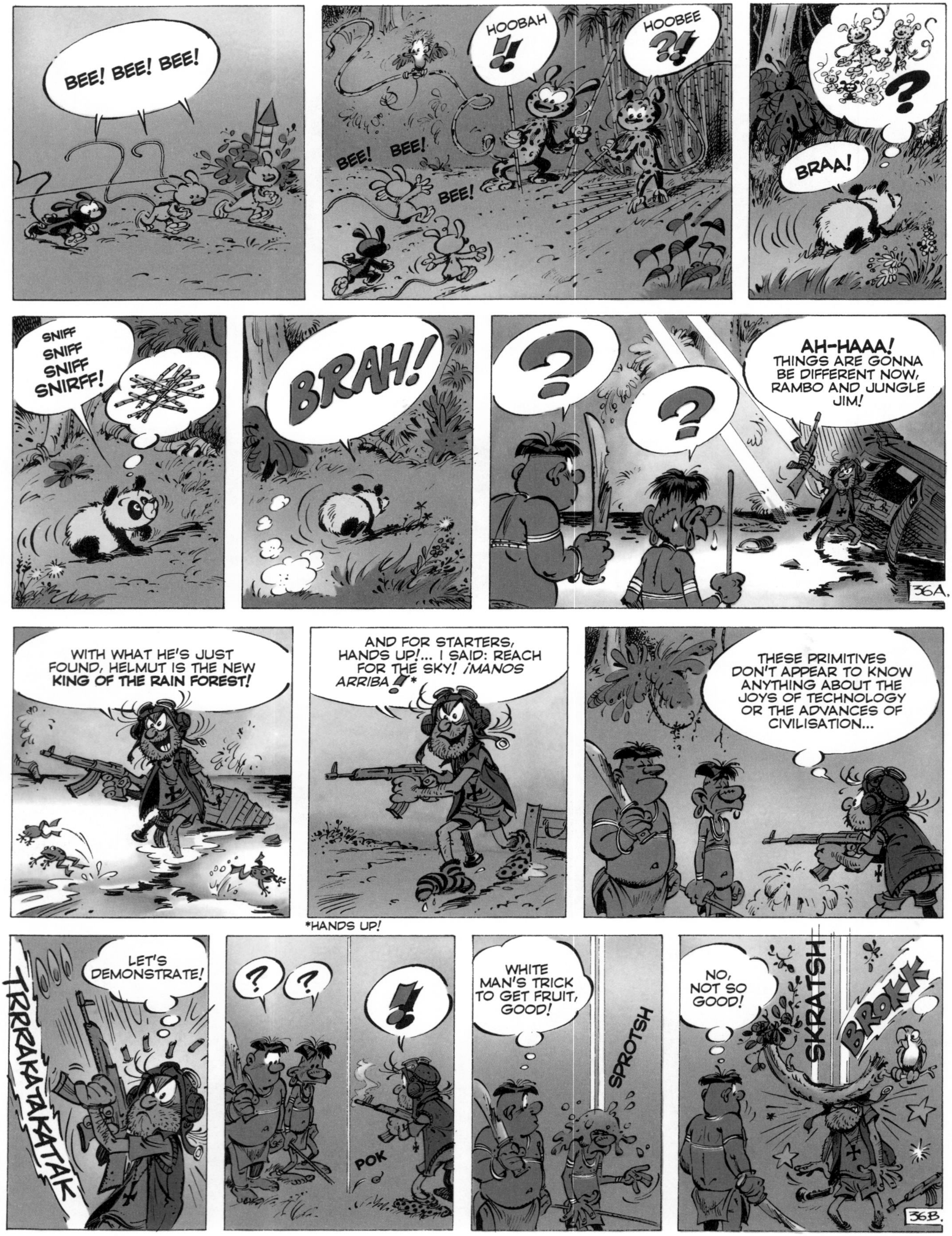
BEE! BEE! BEE!
HOOBAH
!
BEE! BEE!
BEE!
HOOBEE
?!
?
BRAA!
SNIFF SNIFF SNIFF SNIRFF!
BRAH!
?
?
AH-HAAA! THINGS ARE GONNA BE DIFFERENT NOW, RAMBO AND JUNGLE JIM!
36A.
WITH WHAT HE'S JUST FOUND, HELMUT IS THE NEW KING OF THE RAIN FOREST!
AND FOR STARTERS, HANDS UP!... I SAID: REACH FOR THE SKY! ¡MANOS ARRIBA!*
THESE PRIMITIVES DON'T APPEAR TO KNOW ANYTHING ABOUT THE JOYS OF TECHNOLOGY OR THE ADVANCES OF CIVILISATION...
*HANDS UP!
TRRRAKATAKATAK
LET'S DEMONSTRATE!
?
?
!
POK
WHITE MAN'S TRICK TO GET FRUIT, GOOD!
SPROTSH
NO, NOT SO GOOD!
SKRATSH
BROKK
36B.

THE REIGN OF THE KING OF THE RAIN FOREST WAS BRIEF...

GRRMBL! SCHMUTZ! GRRMBL!

ZZZZ

BRAH!!

BRAH BRAH BRAH

HOOBRAH! ER... HOOBAH!

BRAH?

BANG PSHEEE PIF PUTT

37A.

HAVOCAS TAH-LEEHOH!

RATAPLAKAPAF PANK WWWWEEEEE PUTT SHSHSCHSHEEEEEWWWW

37B.

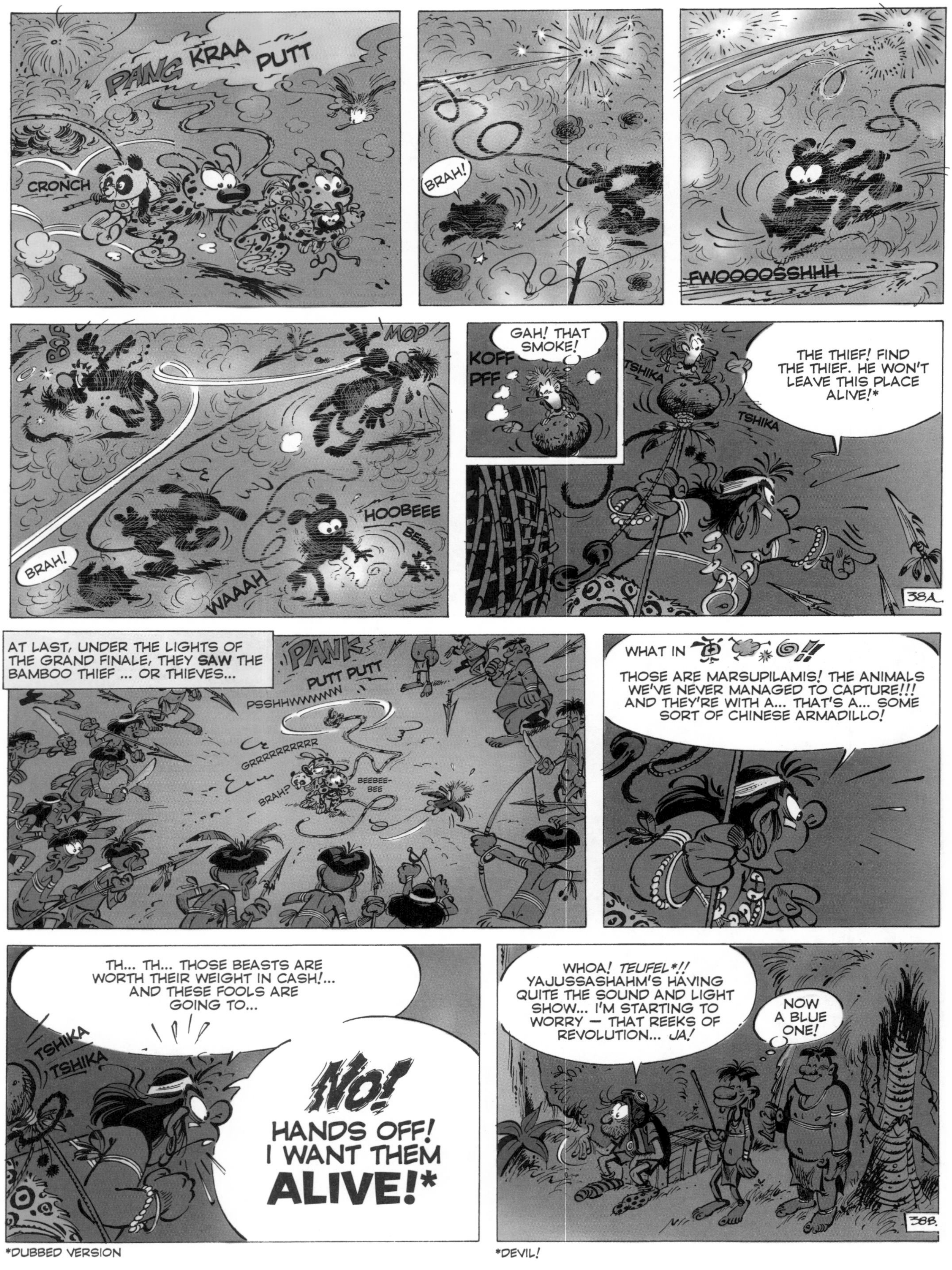
PANG KRAA PUTT
CRONCH
BRAH!
FWOOOOSSHHH
MOP
BRAH!
HOOBEEE
WAAAH
GAH! THAT SMOKE!
KOFF
PFF
TSHIKA
TSHIKA
THE THIEF! FIND THE THIEF. HE WON'T LEAVE THIS PLACE ALIVE!*
AT LAST, UNDER THE LIGHTS OF THE GRAND FINALE, THEY SAW THE BAMBOO THIEF ... OR THIEVES...
PANK
PUTT PUTT
PSSHHWWWWW
GRRRRRRRRRR
BRAH?
BEEBEE-BEE
WHAT IN
THOSE ARE MARSUPILAMIS! THE ANIMALS WE'VE NEVER MANAGED TO CAPTURE!!! AND THEY'RE WITH A... THAT'S A... SOME SORT OF CHINESE ARMADILLO!
TH... TH... THOSE BEASTS ARE WORTH THEIR WEIGHT IN CASH!... AND THESE FOOLS ARE GOING TO...
TSHIKA
TSHIKA
NO! HANDS OFF! I WANT THEM ALIVE!*
WHOA! TEUFEL*!! YAJUSSASHAHM'S HAVING QUITE THE SOUND AND LIGHT SHOW... I'M STARTING TO WORRY — THAT REEKS OF REVOLUTION... JA!
NOW A BLUE ONE!

*DUBBED VERSION

*DEVIL!

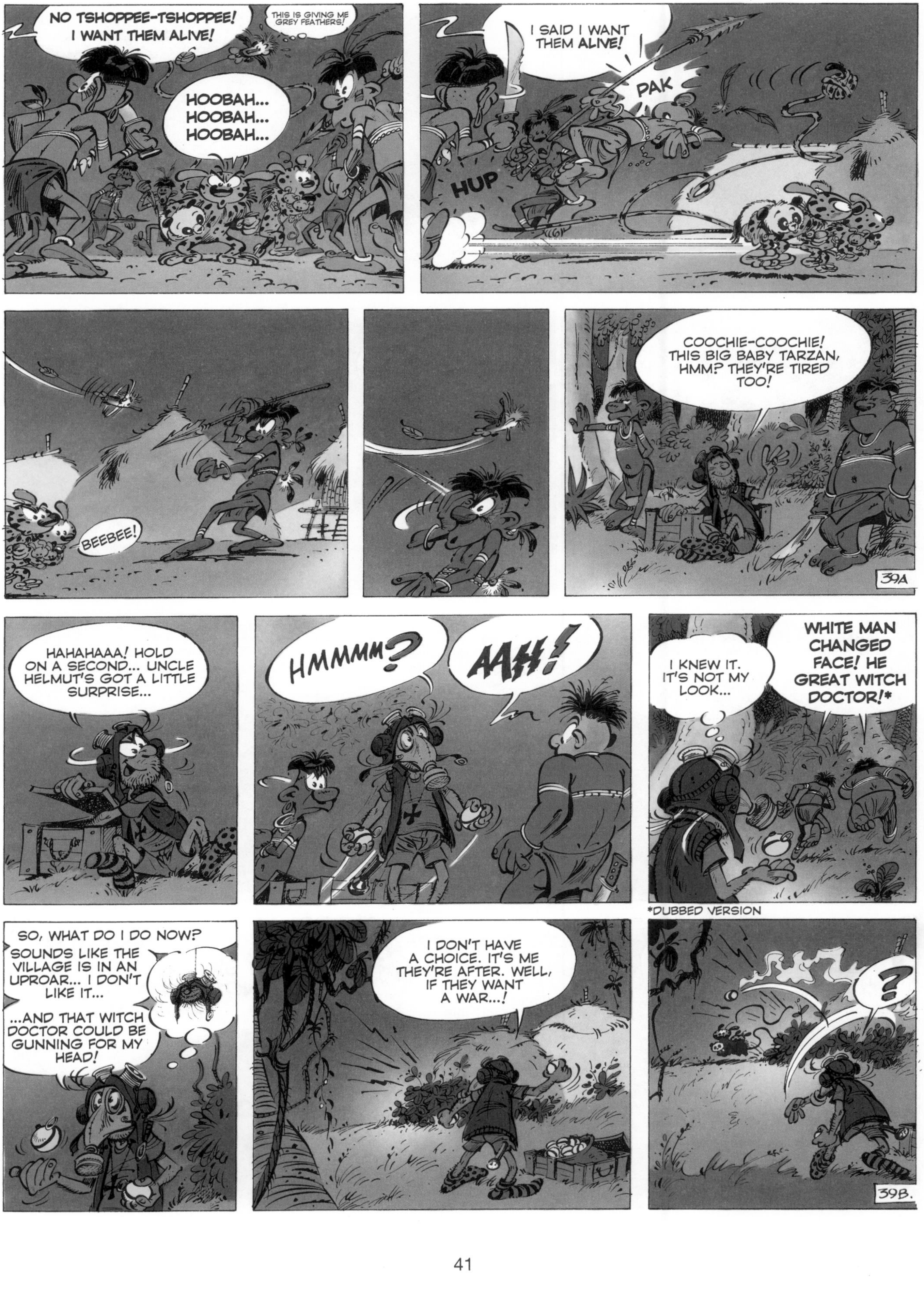
NO TSHOPPEE-TSHOPPEE! I WANT THEM ALIVE!
THIS IS GIVING ME GREY FEATHERS!
HOOBAH... HOOBAH... HOOBAH...
I SAID I WANT THEM ALIVE!
PAK
HUP
BEEBEE!
COOCHIE-COOCHIE! THIS BIG BABY TARZAN, HMM? THEY'RE TIRED TOO!
39A
HAHAHAAA! HOLD ON A SECOND... UNCLE HELMUT'S GOT A LITTLE SURPRISE...
HMMMM?
AAH!
I KNEW IT. IT'S NOT MY LOOK...
WHITE MAN CHANGED FACE! HE GREAT WITCH DOCTOR!*
SO, WHAT DO I DO NOW? SOUNDS LIKE THE VILLAGE IS IN AN UPROAR... I DON'T LIKE IT...
...AND THAT WITCH DOCTOR COULD BE GUNNING FOR MY HEAD!
I DON'T HAVE A CHOICE. IT'S ME THEY'RE AFTER. WELL, IF THEY WANT A WAR...!
?
39B.
*DUBBED VERSION

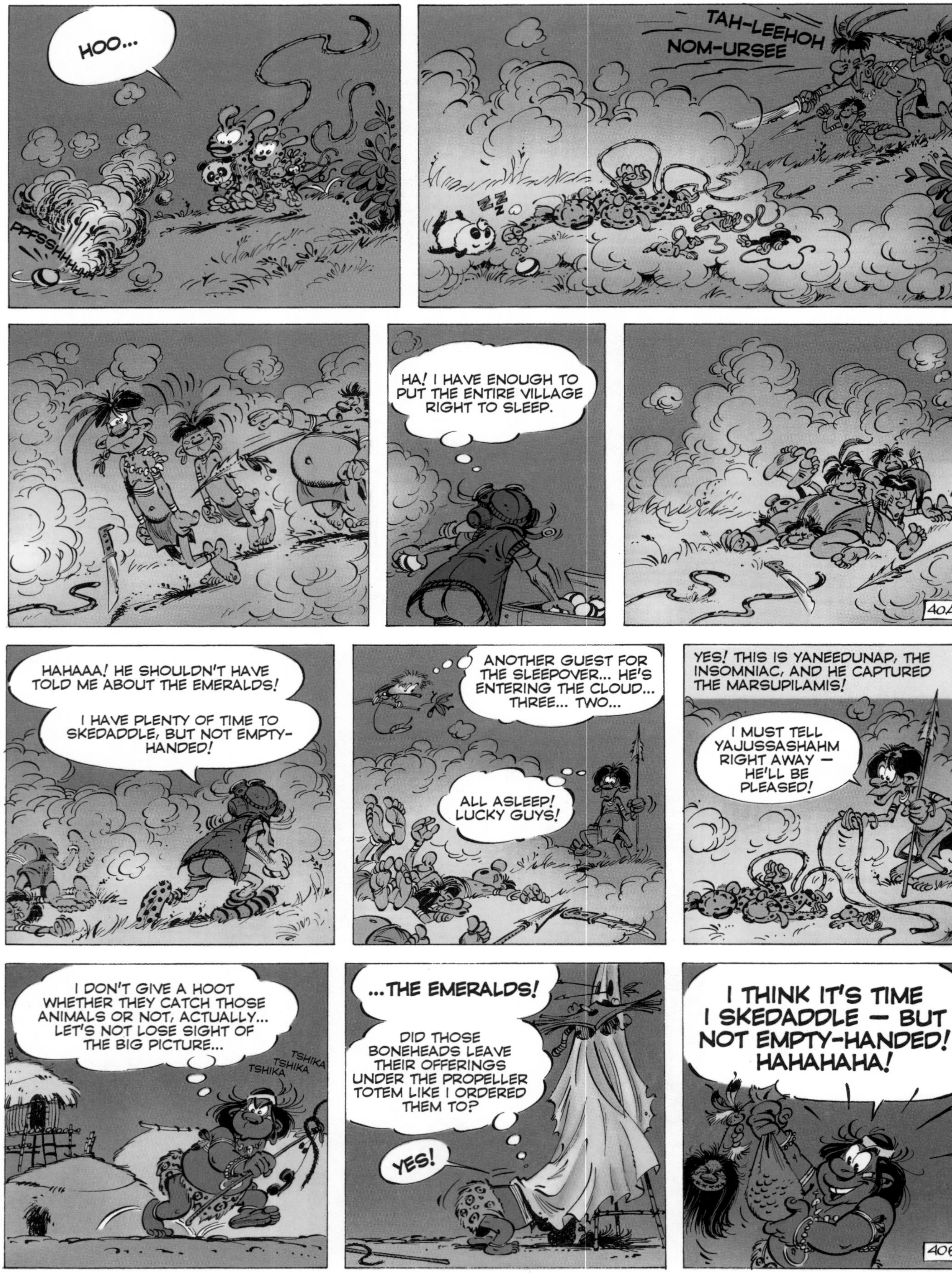
HOO...
PPFSSHHHHH
TAH-LEEHOH
NOM-URSEE
ZZZ
HA! I HAVE ENOUGH TO PUT THE ENTIRE VILLAGE RIGHT TO SLEEP.
40A.
HAHAAA! HE SHOULDN'T HAVE TOLD ME ABOUT THE EMERALDS!
I HAVE PLENTY OF TIME TO SKEDADDLE, BUT NOT EMPTY-HANDED!
ANOTHER GUEST FOR THE SLEEPOVER... HE'S ENTERING THE CLOUD... THREE... TWO...
ALL ASLEEP! LUCKY GUYS!
YES! THIS IS YANEEDUNAP, THE INSOMNIAC, AND HE CAPTURED THE MARSUPILAMIS!
I MUST TELL YAJUSSASHAHM RIGHT AWAY — HE'LL BE PLEASED!
I DON'T GIVE A HOOT WHETHER THEY CATCH THOSE ANIMALS OR NOT, ACTUALLY... LET'S NOT LOSE SIGHT OF THE BIG PICTURE...
TSHIKA TSHIKA TSHIKA
...THE EMERALDS!
DID THOSE BONEHEADS LEAVE THEIR OFFERINGS UNDER THE PROPELLER TOTEM LIKE I ORDERED THEM TO?
YES!
I THINK IT'S TIME I SKEDADDLE — BUT NOT EMPTY-HANDED! HAHAHAHA!
40B.

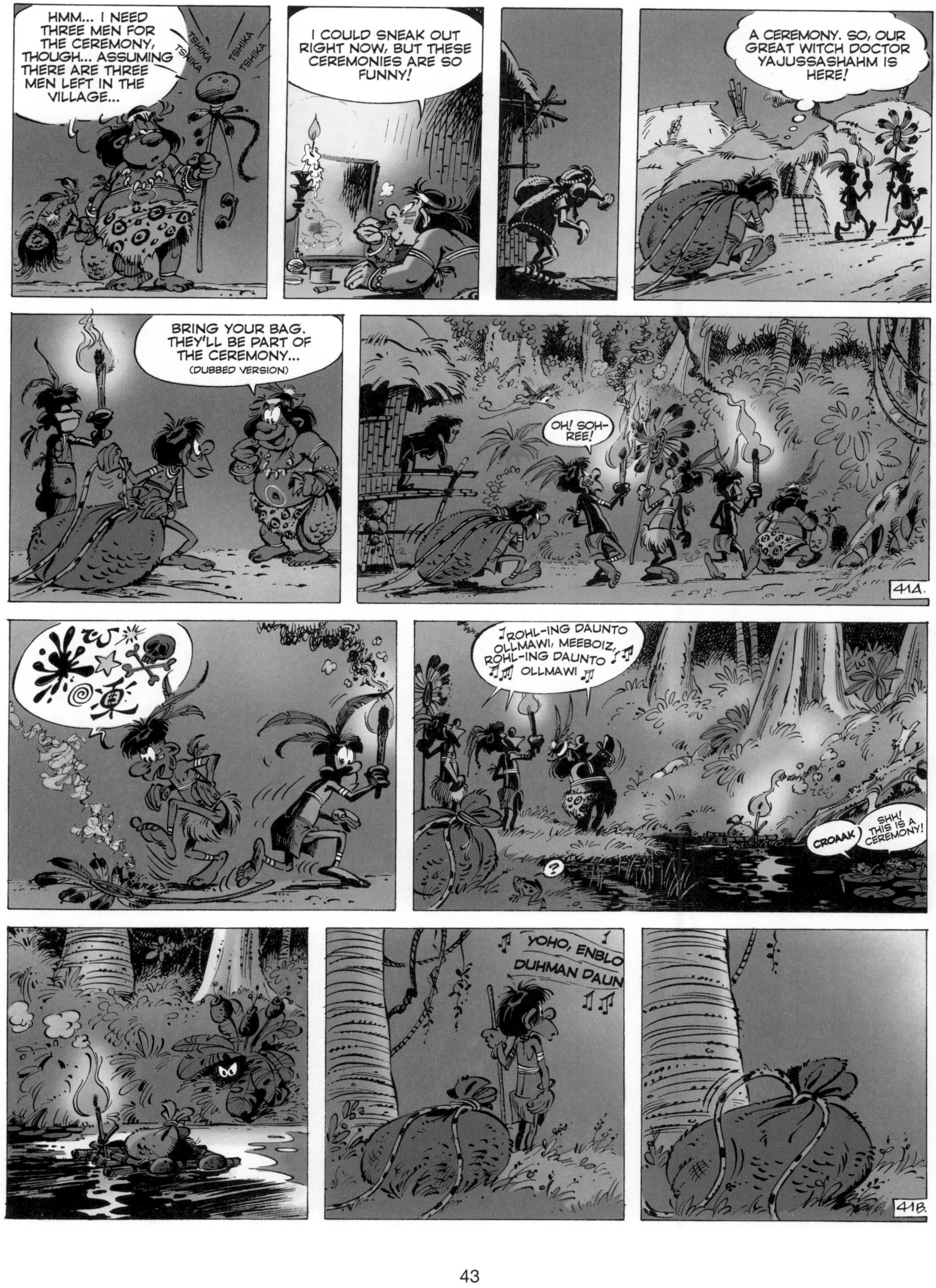
HMM... I NEED THREE MEN FOR THE CEREMONY, THOUGH... ASSUMING THERE ARE THREE MEN LEFT IN THE VILLAGE...
TSHIKA TSHIKA TSHIKA TSHIKA
I COULD SNEAK OUT RIGHT NOW, BUT THESE CEREMONIES ARE SO FUNNY!
A CEREMONY. SO, OUR GREAT WITCH DOCTOR YAJUSSASHAHM IS HERE!
BRING YOUR BAG. THEY'LL BE PART OF THE CEREMONY... (DUBBED VERSION)
OH! SOH-REE!
41A.
ROHL-ING DAUNTO OLLMAWI, MEEBOIZ, ROHL-ING DAUNTO OLLMAWI
CROAK
SHH! THIS IS A CEREMONY!
YOHO, ENBLO DUHMAN DAUN
41B.

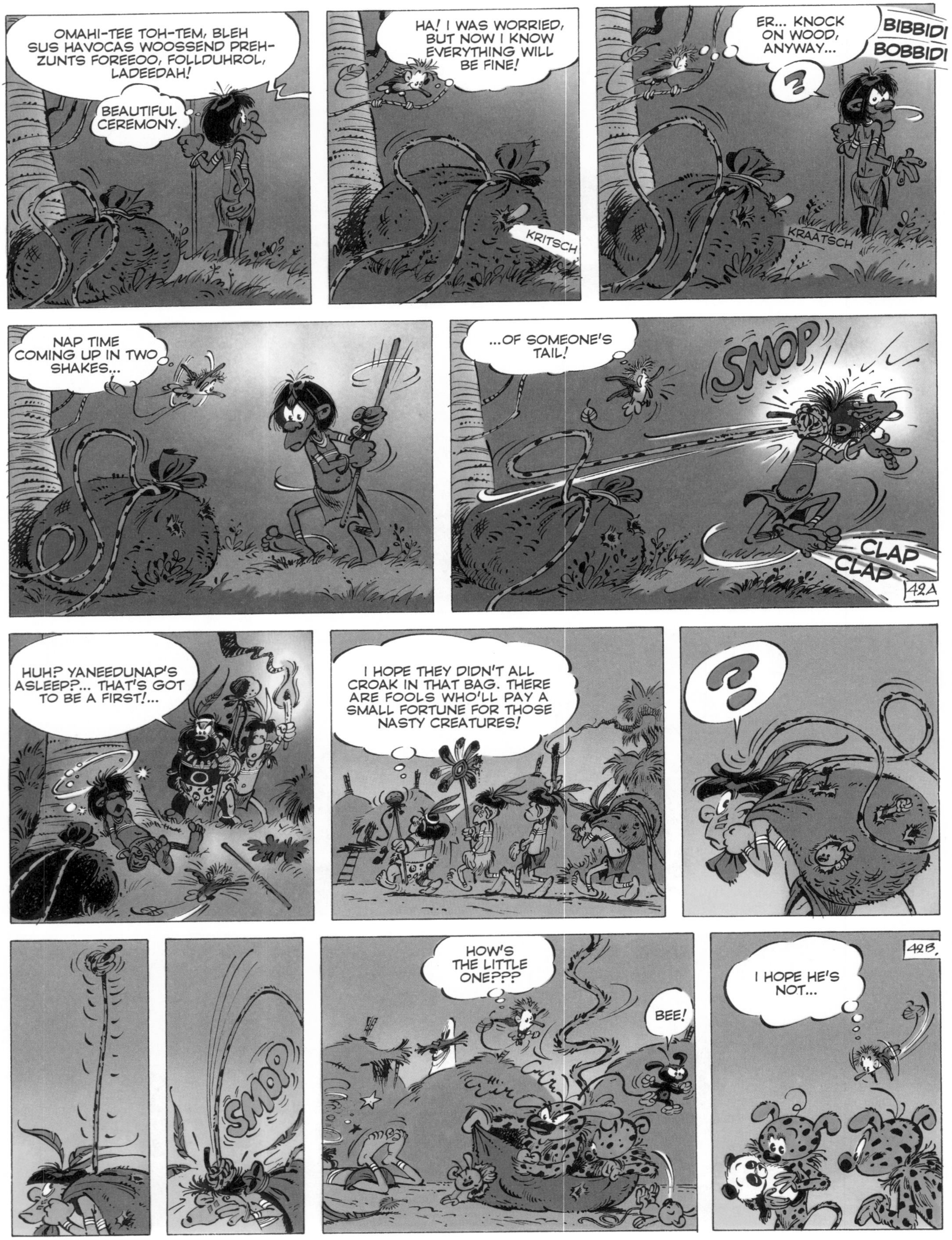

OMAHI-TEE TOH-TEM, BLEH SUS HAVOCAS WOOSSEND PREH-ZUNTS FOREEOO, FOLLDUHROL, LADEEDAH!
BEAUTIFUL CEREMONY.
HA! I WAS WORRIED, BUT NOW I KNOW EVERYTHING WILL BE FINE!
KRITSCH
ER... KNOCK ON WOOD, ANYWAY...
BIBBIDI
BOBBIDI
?
KRAATSCH
NAP TIME COMING UP IN TWO SHAKES...
...OF SOMEONE'S TAIL!
SMOP
CLAP
CLAP
42A
HUH? YANEEDUNAP'S ASLEEP?... THAT'S GOT TO BE A FIRST!...
I HOPE THEY DIDN'T ALL CROAK IN THAT BAG. THERE ARE FOOLS WHO'LL PAY A SMALL FORTUNE FOR THOSE NASTY CREATURES!
?
SMOP
HOW'S THE LITTLE ONE???
BEE!
42B
I HOPE HE'S NOT...

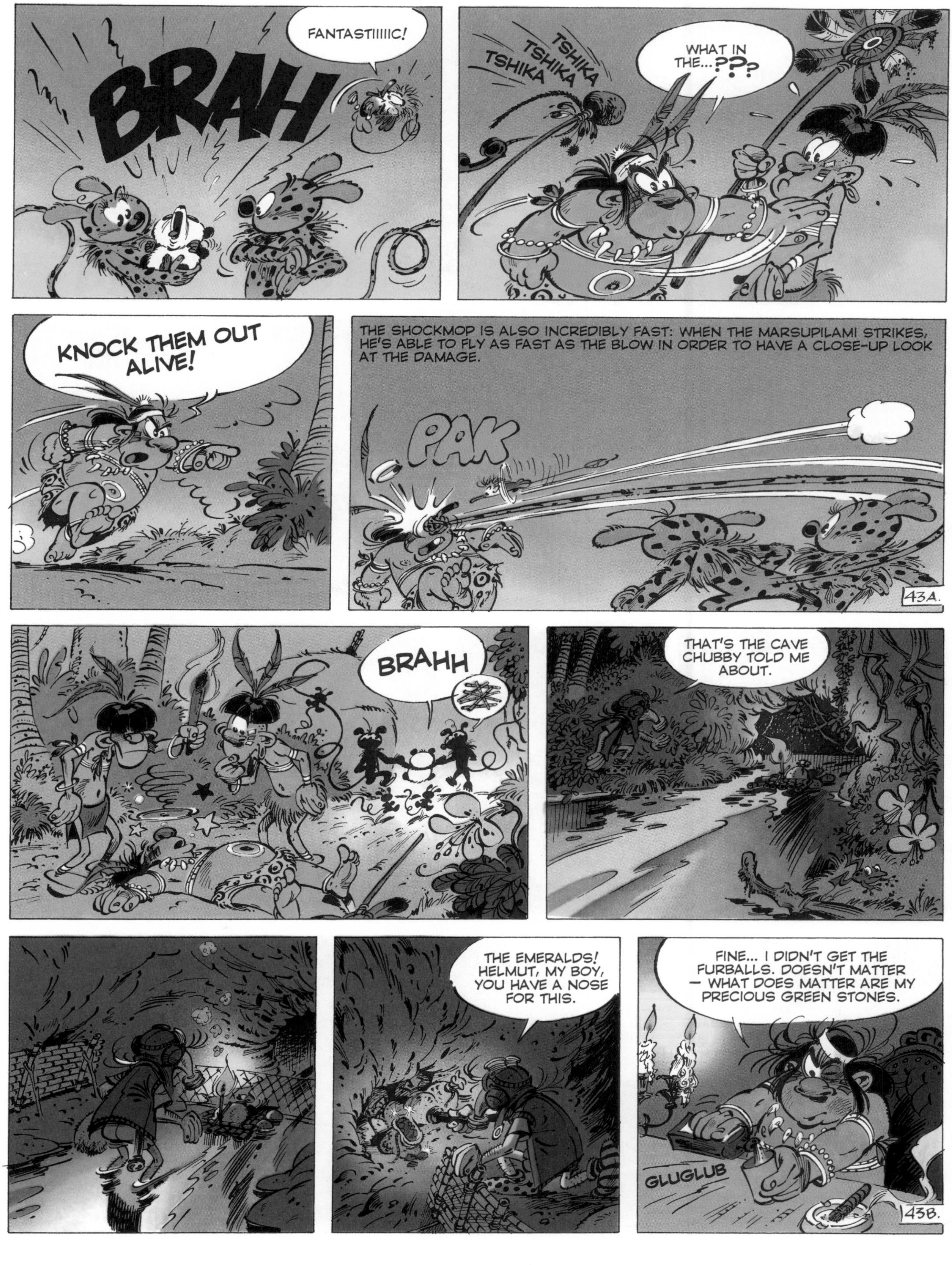
FANTASTIIIIIC!
BRAH
TSHIKA TSHIKA TSHIKA
WHAT IN THE...???
KNOCK THEM OUT ALIVE!
THE SHOCKMOP IS ALSO INCREDIBLY FAST: WHEN THE MARSUPILAMI STRIKES, HE'S ABLE TO FLY AS FAST AS THE BLOW IN ORDER TO HAVE A CLOSE-UP LOOK AT THE DAMAGE.
PAK
43A.
BRAHH
THAT'S THE CAVE CHUBBY TOLD ME ABOUT.
THE EMERALDS! HELMUT, MY BOY, YOU HAVE A NOSE FOR THIS.
FINE... I DIDN'T GET THE FURBALLS. DOESN'T MATTER — WHAT DOES MATTER ARE MY PRECIOUS GREEN STONES.
GLUGLUB
43B.

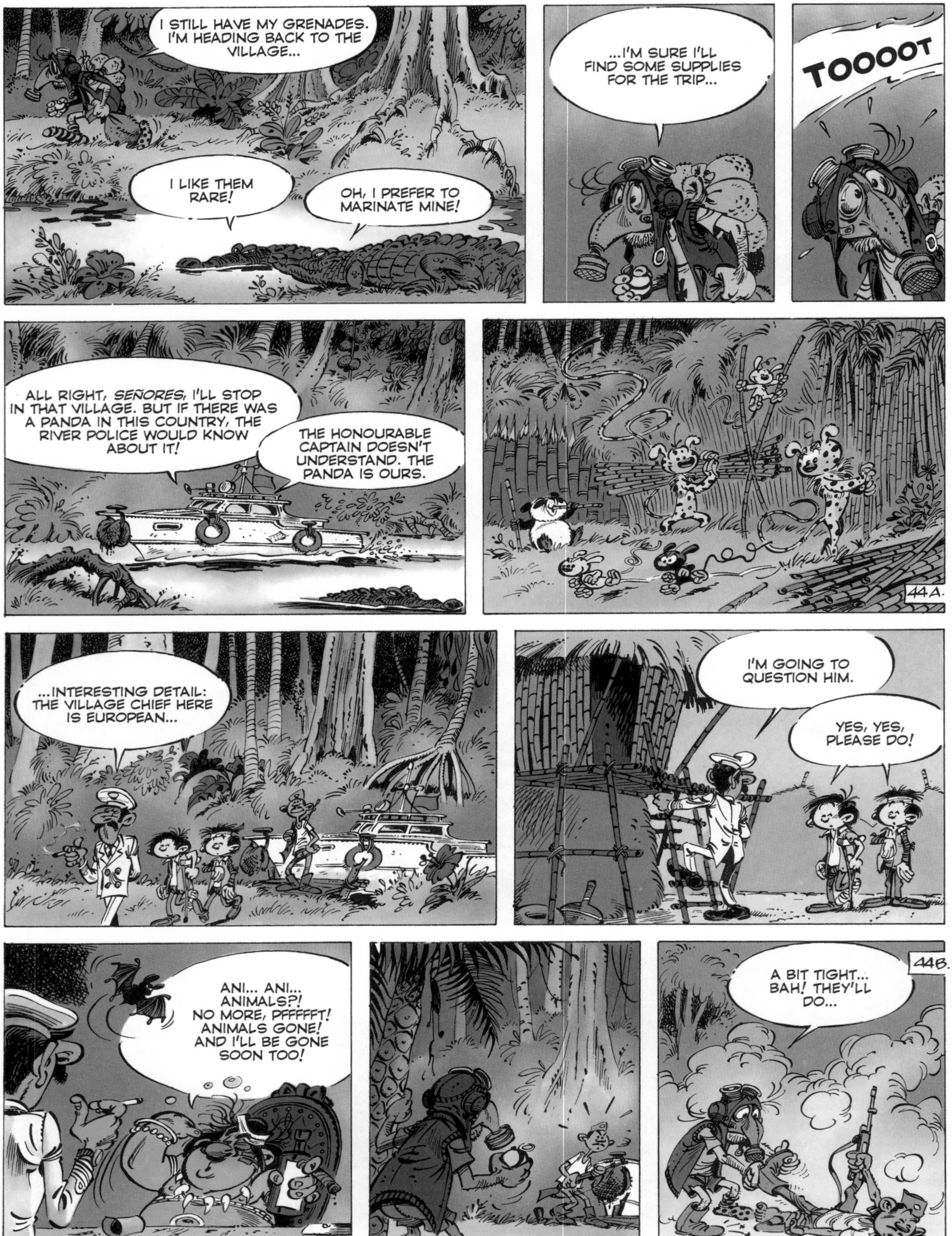
I STILL HAVE MY GRENADES. I'M HEADING BACK TO THE VILLAGE...
I LIKE THEM RARE!
OH, I PREFER TO MARINATE MINE!
...I'M SURE I'LL FIND SOME SUPPLIES FOR THE TRIP...
TOOOOT
ALL RIGHT, SEÑORES, I'LL STOP IN THAT VILLAGE. BUT IF THERE WAS A PANDA IN THIS COUNTRY, THE RIVER POLICE WOULD KNOW ABOUT IT!
THE HONOURABLE CAPTAIN DOESN'T UNDERSTAND. THE PANDA IS OURS.
44A.
...INTERESTING DETAIL: THE VILLAGE CHIEF HERE IS EUROPEAN...
I'M GOING TO QUESTION HIM.
YES, YES, PLEASE DO!
ANI... ANI... ANIMALS?! NO MORE, PFFFFFT! ANIMALS GONE! AND I'LL BE GONE SOON TOO!
44B.
A BIT TIGHT... BAH! THEY'LL DO...

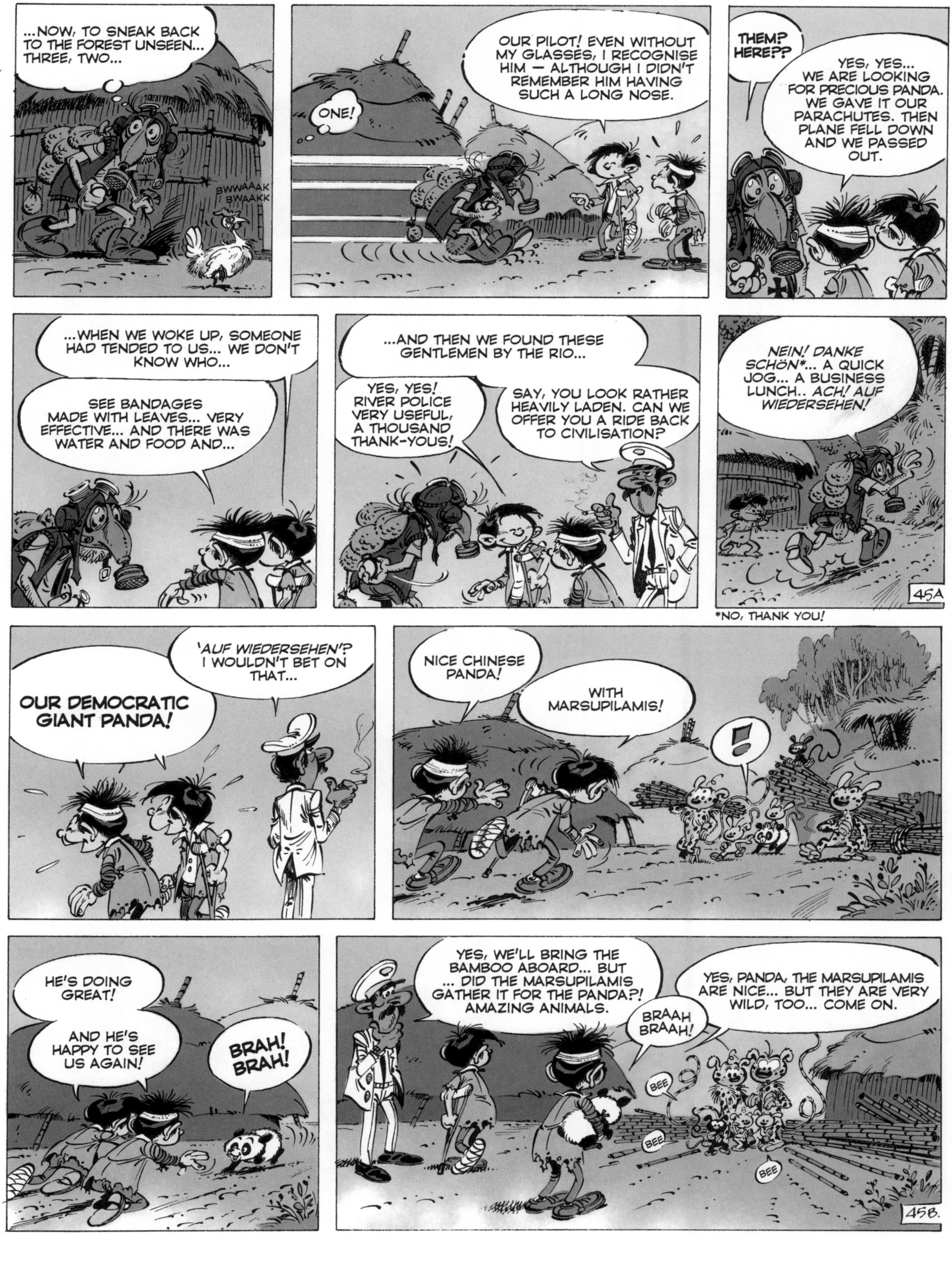

...NOW, TO SNEAK BACK TO THE FOREST UNSEEN... THREE, TWO...
BWWAAAK BWAAKK
ONE!
OUR PILOT! EVEN WITHOUT MY GLASSES, I RECOGNISE HIM — ALTHOUGH I DIDN'T REMEMBER HIM HAVING SUCH A LONG NOSE.
THEM? HERE??
YES, YES... WE ARE LOOKING FOR PRECIOUS PANDA. WE GAVE IT OUR PARACHUTES. THEN PLANE FELL DOWN AND WE PASSED OUT.
...WHEN WE WOKE UP, SOMEONE HAD TENDED TO US... WE DON'T KNOW WHO...
SEE BANDAGES MADE WITH LEAVES... VERY EFFECTIVE... AND THERE WAS WATER AND FOOD AND...
...AND THEN WE FOUND THESE GENTLEMEN BY THE RIO...
YES, YES! RIVER POLICE VERY USEFUL, A THOUSAND THANK-YOUS!
SAY, YOU LOOK RATHER HEAVILY LADEN. CAN WE OFFER YOU A RIDE BACK TO CIVILISATION?
NEIN! DANKE SCHÖN*... A QUICK JOG... A BUSINESS LUNCH.. ACH! AUF WIEDERSEHEN!
45A
*NO, THANK YOU!
OUR DEMOCRATIC GIANT PANDA!
'AUF WIEDERSEHEN'? I WOULDN'T BET ON THAT...
NICE CHINESE PANDA!
WITH MARSUPILAMIS!
HE'S DOING GREAT!
AND HE'S HAPPY TO SEE US AGAIN!
BRAH! BRAH!
YES, WE'LL BRING THE BAMBOO ABOARD... BUT ... DID THE MARSUPILAMIS GATHER IT FOR THE PANDA?! AMAZING ANIMALS.
BRAAH BRAAH!
YES, PANDA, THE MARSUPILAMIS ARE NICE... BUT THEY ARE VERY WILD, TOO... COME ON.
BEE
BEE
BEE
45B.

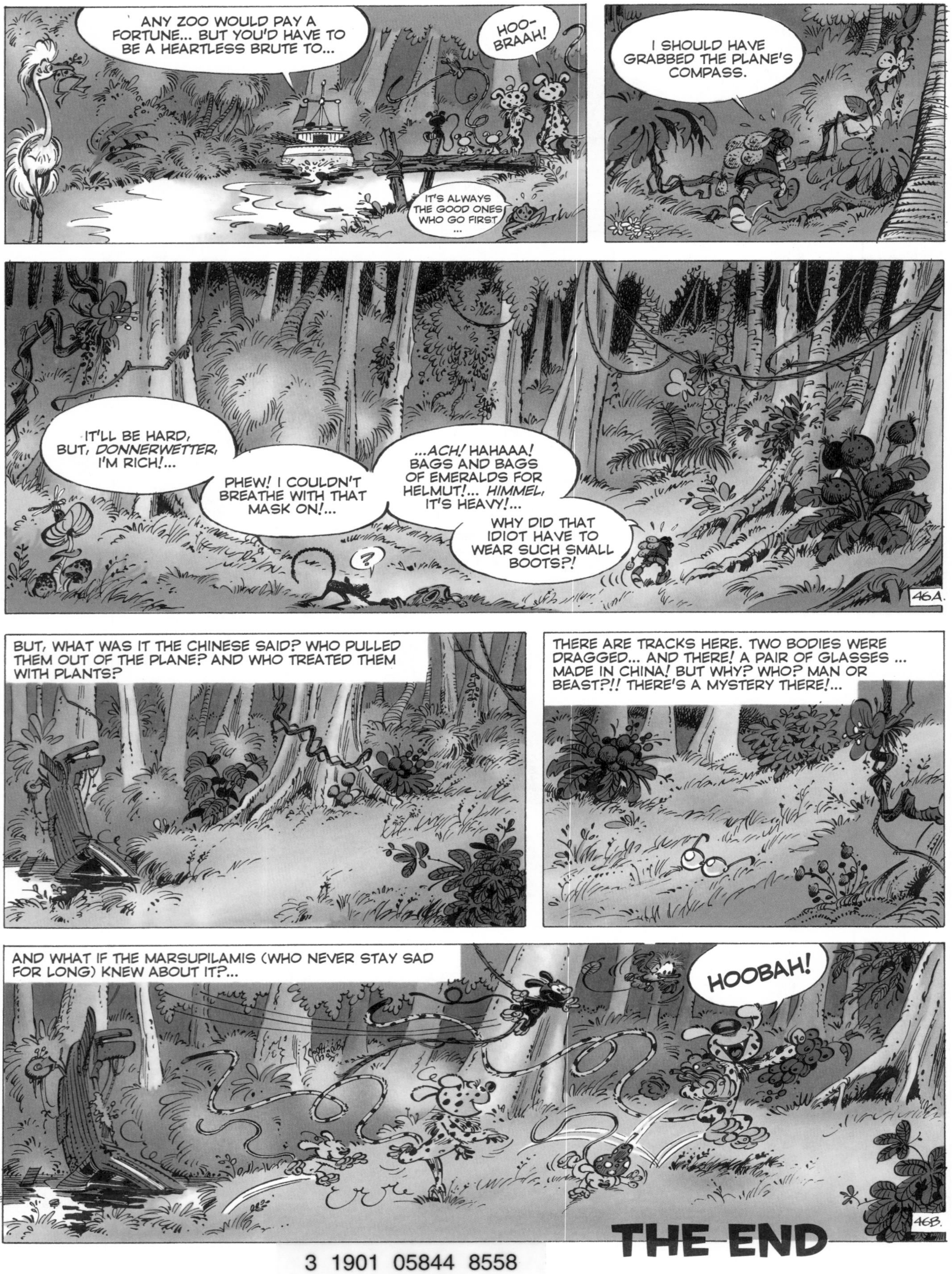
ANY ZOO WOULD PAY A FORTUNE... BUT YOU'D HAVE TO BE A HEARTLESS BRUTE TO...
HOO-BRAAH!
IT'S ALWAYS THE GOOD ONES WHO GO FIRST ...
I SHOULD HAVE GRABBED THE PLANE'S COMPASS.
IT'LL BE HARD, BUT, *DONNERWETTER*, I'M RICH!...
PHEW! I COULDN'T BREATHE WITH THAT MASK ON!...
...*ACH!* HAHAAA! BAGS AND BAGS OF EMERALDS FOR HELMUT!... *HIMMEL*, IT'S HEAVY!...
WHY DID THAT IDIOT HAVE TO WEAR SUCH SMALL BOOTS?!
?
46A.
BUT, WHAT WAS IT THE CHINESE SAID? WHO PULLED THEM OUT OF THE PLANE? AND WHO TREATED THEM WITH PLANTS?
THERE ARE TRACKS HERE. TWO BODIES WERE DRAGGED... AND THERE! A PAIR OF GLASSES ... MADE IN CHINA! BUT WHY? WHO? MAN OR BEAST?!! THERE'S A MYSTERY THERE!...
AND WHAT IF THE MARSUPILAMIS (WHO NEVER STAY SAD FOR LONG) KNEW ABOUT IT?...
HOOBAH!
46B.

THE END